A NEED FOR CHARLIE

A NOVEL

By: CHRISTIAN KOEGEL

A Grass Valley Group Publication.

Grass Valley Press Inc.
Woodbury, MN 55125

ISBN-13: 978-0-578-00694-9

Art & cover design by Philip Westfall © 2008.

Manufactured in the United States of America.

For Carrie, who showed me the way.

1

"Asleep in the Desert"

"So what have you got?" Aspen asked with a certain depravity. He fiddled with his aviator style sunglasses, trying desperately without much success to keep them snug against his face.

Detective Tucker, his partner, grinned deeply at him despite the scorching late September sun. These two always seemed to have an ulterior motive when talking to one another. They were good partners. Never were they really at odds. Still, it was evident to everyone from the district attorney to the medical examiner that they never were too friendly with one another. Anyone who ever took part in or overheard them in their conversations automatically detected the double speak. The kind that two fellas who weren't comfortable with one another would engage in.

Plus, they had always given the appearance to be in direct competition with one another. Who could crack the coldest lead? Who could determine the next course of investigation the quickest? Who could extract the most useful information from a witness? But despite the games they would play, the kind with unspoken rules and unfounded origins, they never left a book open. Since they became partners eight years previous, not one case had ever been tossed aside unresolved. This was precisely why their secret and separate requests to be transferred to the chief would go unfulfilled.

You two – you gel together perfectly. No Sergeant worth their salt would split up a team like you two. Lettalone me, he once quipped to Aspen.

Aspen, taking a cue from the stranger he called his partner, surveyed the scene again. Not much there beside Route 70. Their mini camp stood smack dab in between Peridot and Cutter – right in the heart of the San Carlos Indian Reservation. Not much there but an overturned pickup truck with bits of broken glass and bent fragmented metal scattered around its sandy crust. About 500 yards down the road was an ugly looking semi tractor-trailer, which Aspen guessed had seen better days. Its grotesque red paint was chipping, and its windshield was caked with dirt and grime. A photographer was snapping a few shots of a presumably dead John that was covered with a sheet, as well as the surrounding area. Beside him, another investigator Aspen thought he recognized as a State dick, he was setting down the numbered plaques, marking evidence.

He shook his head vigorously at his partner, "I don't see anything interesting."

"Really? Then let me enlighten you. Mr. Doe under the sheet there has yet to be identified, found him next to the pickup. Now the sun's only been up for six hours, but this guy smells like he's been dead for six years. Looks it too. Then Farve came by and confirmed it. You just missed him. It was a preliminary theory, sure. But he took one look at the guy and said, 'no way this guy died last night.' He told me a week at least, maybe more. They took him to county and will do the tox report when they can fit it in. But he didn't think there was any foul play, which I don't need to tell you is why they'll do it when they can fit it in. Apparently a whole mess of people were killed in Gila County this past week. Did you hear about the kid in Globe? Ingested the arsenic that was in his cereal, they suspect one or both of the parents. Same with the meth lab that blew up in that trailer down in Cutter? Yeah, they have their hands full this week."

"Look, I don't have time for this. I just rode 40 miles from Tonto Park. I had to ask the driver to stop three times to piss, because of my infection. So lay it on me," Aspen's impatient, crooked face crowed to his partner.

The grin had eased from Tucker's mouth momentarily. "What were you doing in Tonto?"

"I told you, Cyndi signed me up to chaperone Bailey's class on a field trip. They take all the third graders and a few saps who signed up to watch over them, cram 'em into a bus with no AC, and ship 'em off to Tonto

National Monument to learn about cacti, snakes and basins. She didn't tell me till two days ago. Thought it was the funniest thing in the world. I told her, you're lucky my sick time is so stocked up, despite my infection,'" he brushed his hand briskly along his crotch to illustrate his point.

The smile returned to Tucker's face, it was followed by a brief, albeit choked up laughter. "Aspen was in Tonto learning about the snakes," he jested to a passing paramedic.

The medic was busy packing up equipment to wheel over to the meatwagon. He didn't understand the joke and stared at Tucker quizzically until he continued to go about his business.

"Forget all that!" Aspen vied for his attention, "I told you not to page me unless it was an emergency. Something that you couldn't handle by yourself. So, I say again, 'what have you got?'"

Tucker's face switched back to game mode, "This one is quite interesting, actually. You should have been here a little sooner, you missed all the excitement."

"I know. I read the news – but back to this. What's the interesting part? And what makes you so sure something happened last night? This is a lonely stretch." Aspen winced at the miles of sand and rugged terrain surrounding the valley they were entrenched in.

"We had a live one. A girl, about fifteen. They rushed her to *Good Samaritan*, and last I heard over the radio is that she's having an emergency Peria-ce-tab-u-lar Os-teo-tomy."

"She's– what's that?"

"I had to ask, but didn't hear anything substantial. From the sounds of it, it's surgery on the hip. But she does have a couple of broken bones and a shattered pelvis. So far as the med told me anyway. She was dehydrated too – of course. But she was able to talk. She told the officers that arrived on the scene that Mr. Doe was driving the truck. They asked her how she knew, she told them that he was up and about last night, talking to her. So therein lies the question. How could a guy who has been so obviously dead for at least a fortnight be up and walking around? And how could a guy well past his expiration date be driving a truck? Last I checked, the dead don't drive."

"Did she say anything else?" Aspen asked with his interest finally piqued.

"They weren't able to get much. Like I said, she was gouged up pretty good. But she's going to make it." Tucker hesitated, but then added, "That's an interview I'm looking forward to."

"Huh." Aspen glanced around, once again surveying the valley. He was listening to what that voice that all natural born dicks are equipped with very early on in life had to say. Some might refer to it as a sixth sense, but Aspen always liked to cite it as the sound of his wheels spinning. "So we got one dead guy, and one live girl. No foul play suspected. Two vehicles, one pedestrian, one heavy artillery. Am I missing anything?"

"What about some obvious ones?" Tucker's grin returned, as their unspoken game had commenced.

"What?" Aspen sighed.

"How the hell did that pickup turn over like that? Why the hell is the semi parked so far away? And why is there not a trace of another person or vehicle in sight? Something or someone has got to be missing. But what?"

"Did you check out the semi yet?"

"No, I thought I'd wait for you."

"Aww gee, thanks."

"Well, you ready?"

Aspen circled his eyes and mind around the scene once more, trying to become as familiar with it as his partner so as not to miss a beat. "Do you think this is going to be the one to break our streak?"

"Man, this is one for the books, I don't really know what to expect." Tucker looked surprised at his partner, as if he had just said something largely arbitrary. But the truth was, and Aspen picked up on it right away, he was probably thinking the same thing. Would this break arguably the best streak in the history of Gila County, Arizona.

"Interesting," Aspen echoed his partner's earlier observation.

"That's what I said," Tucker replied.

<u>2</u>

"Meet the New Boss"

Charlie Coldbrick ambled up the rusted stairwell, leading to the upper office of 1609 Benson Road. He climbed the stairs like he was climbing a mountain; slow and methodically. He was tired. He knew his extended vacation wouldn't have lasted forever. What he didn't know was that his triumphant return to work would start so listlessly. The way Charlie figured it was he had been away too long and had gotten too used to normal nine-to-five hours– a dangerous habit for someone in his profession to undertake.

He had meant to stay up late two nights previous, that way he would have lounged around and slept most of the following day away. But after three weeks of steady, healthy sleep, his body had gotten spoiled.

Still, he wasn't going to change his routine because of the lack of a little shut-eye. That was something he was just going to have to deal with. After all, he had always started his trips at night, he'd be damned if any amount of news or temporary leave of his senses was going to change that.

He placed one foot on the first step of the thin, metal staircase leading up to Hal's office and the exhaustion had hit him already. Old Hal had been Charlie's boss ever since 1979. He came in around the same time the DOT bears vowed to clean up the industry. Charlie stifled out a laugh, which caused a nasty piece of inner lung to get lodged in his throat, that was until he hawked and spat it back out.

He wasn't able to go up yet, he needed more time before he started this trip. Savagely, he scratched his face before he came out with a Red. He lit it up quickly and paced as he smoked. Every so often, he snuck a glance up at the office window. The light was still on up there, and its dim shadow could be seen merging with the light of the setting sun.

Old Hal's working late again, he imagined. *Of course, who can blame him when he has to go home to that leeching sow of a woman.*

Charlie had met Lacey, Hal's wife, once at a company barbeque out in Saddle Springs, Colorado. He never figured for the life of him why a decent man like Hal would have wanted to be married. That and other matters briefly passed through Charlie's mind as he hacked and smoked his Red. He also worked the prep plans out in his head (it had been a while).

Make it to Grand Island before I have to rest. Gas up at that station where Mickey Calhoun almost lost his leg refixin' his trailer, dumbshit forgot to chock his wheels. Drive a few more, catch some zzz's and be in Colorado by morning. And from there –

From there, it was on to rotten Tempe, Arizona.

That's one thing Charlie didn't understand, he had been pondering it the last couple of weeks. Why would old Hal give him a run to Tempe his first trip back in over three weeks? That may've been part of the reason why Charlie was so hesitant to start up those stairs, he was afraid of the answer. Things moved quite swiftly in Charlie's industry, maybe he was afraid the pace car had finally lapped him.

He stubbed his Red out with more force than he thought he retained. Seeing the orange, errant ashes burn out and spiral into the windy landscape comforted him for some reason. Strangely enough, it was the perfect symbol for why he got into this business in the first place. He wanted to blow in the wind just like the ashes of a freshly discarded cigarette on the highway. Those highways were his playground back in the old days, he figured maybe they could be again.

Although, as Charlie had gotten on in years, the need to play had faded a bit. It was gradual at first, but then it evolved faster and faster. As he earned more vacation time he felt the need to burn it up. Nothing like his most recent tour, just a few days here and there. But he never knew what to do with himself. He'd mostly spend it at the *Wheelborrow Lounge*, a seedy bar that offered any real entertainment to truckers and bikers only. Many nights he would perch himself on his barstool, drinking seven-seven's and cursing the world along with the rest of them.

He'd do that or he'd sit in his one bedroom apartment off route 408. Counting the number of times the wind would shriek when a rig would pass by. With each tractor wagon that passed, he knew he was that much closer to getting back out to his playground. Closer to feeling the wind fly beneath his feet, closer to greasing up the fifth wheels of American industry. He never knew what to do with himself.

Every so often, he would try more subdued activities. He tried a movie at the mall once, but he found it too damn frustrating on account of all the crowds. Once he even braved a play at a local community theater. That was until he walked out halfway through: the story was ridiculous and he had been itching for a Red ever since he sat down in the cramped, battered seat. They wedged him next to a fat lady and a faggy little banker he knew from town who proceeded to blubber before Act two had even started.

Mostly he had kept to himself.

Every once in a while, the fellas were in town all at the same time and they'd get together for a card game; Thompkins, dirty Sam, Rhiney, even big maple Pete. (They called him big maple Pete on account of Rhiney and his cousin once caught him humping a hole, which turned out to be a critter's nest in a maple tree). But he hadn't seen or heard from any of those characters in what had been going on three years. Charlie would usually end up at the *Wheelborrow*, or a liquor store and wind up getting a greasy pizza for the night.

However, this last time had been different. The few weeks before, Charlie had seen his date book so full it was nearly in the red. Appointments, examinations, a brief meeting with his insurance agent and an even briefer one with his lawyer. It annoyed him to be so busy when he wasn't working. It was supposed to be his vacation and it flew by in a flash. On top of all that, he had to hump down to Tempe, Arizona in the middle of what seemed like the most blazing summer in ten years. Here it was nearing nine PM and it had only slipped back down to ninety-nine degrees.

Charlie contemplated hard as he ascended the stairs slowly, briefly itching his face until he remembered not to. Why wasn't he looking forward to this trip? He couldn't remember even one time where he hadn't been looking forward to getting back out there. He had a sinking feeling that he was making the wrong decision somehow, even though it was the only constant decision he ever made. It all seemed to be getting off on the wrong foot, even if he hadn't been getting off anywhere yet.

He opened the door to the outer office, passed the dozen or so scruffy road atlas's that were borrowed to the new guys until they came to their senses and bought their own, and squelched through the inner door to come face to face with his boss.

"Where's Hal?" he asked, cranky to be staring into the eyes of a thick, yet robust middle-aged woman. She wore a denim jean jacket and a pair of greased, olive cargo pants. She looked at Charlie through eyes that were bitter, if not a little tired. They, like Charlie's, had the sting of being up a trifle too late the previous night.

"Since when did Hal hire hisself a secretary?" Charlie became calmer after he thought he had this most unwelcome visitor sized up.

That was when her eyes seared, they seared like the sun was about to sear Charlie once again. "You Charlie?" she ignored his question.

"Who wants to know?"

"Darla, your new boss, wants to know something all right. Darla wants to know why you're twelve hours late for work. I sent ya the papers over a week ago, it said specifically nine o'clock. Where were ya?"

Although tired, Charlie still took a step back. For a moment he thought he had wandered into the wrong office. He had a slight itch to ask this bull dyke if he was at 1609 Benson Road. But she had mentioned the papers, he remembered briefly glancing at them and then tossing them aside. Whenever he'd find them in his box after some time off, he only looked for one thing – the destination. And the past week's papers said Tempe, Arizona. Everything else had been the same old shit he'd been reading for countless years. The trip number, the tractor and trailer number, the date due, and the shipper. Hal had always kept things nice and consistent, he'd give Charlie the same tractor every time, the due date was predictable enough, it would only be one of three shippers, and the only bastards that would give two shits about the trip number were the dirty, DOT dogs. Nevertheless, he had planned on studying those papers a bit closer once he got his bags into his rig.

Charlie glanced around the office, it looked the same for the most part. The water cooler had moved, and the piles of papers were in neater piles, but piles nonetheless. Strange thing though, every sign of Hal was missing. The electronic dartboard he had set up across from the one window in the building that overlooked the yard. The empty cigar box on the one bare corner of the desk that Hal only kept around because of the naked ladies spread across it. Even the one picture of Hal's pig of a wife, Lacey, had vanished. This butch had told him she was the new boss. Charlie grimaced at the thought, but it was looking like she was telling the truth.

"Well? Where were ya?" her eyes pierced his face for the first time and something in them retreated a little. She might have even flushed up and looked away, but still demanded an answer for his tardiness.

Charlie never wanted to scratch his face as badly as that moment. But the brittle sound of his yellow fingernails scraping away at reptile skin was enough to deter him for the time being. This lady began to pity him and was even feeling remorse for her harsh, stern words. That had angered him more than anything else. "Hal always let me come in at night."

Her eyes lightened up a bit, but her words were still unyielding, she shook her head. "Hal's gone now. I'm here and I wanted this load out by nine…AM!"

"I only leave at night," Charlie persisted, but he felt even more tired. He wanted to get back on the road, anything would've been better than to chew fat with this woman.

"Not anymore, you don't. You leave at the time the papers say."

"I'll be on my way then."

"Hold on a minute – I need the keys to the five speed."

"What in the hell for?"

"You're taking the ten. Jarvis took the five down to Florida, it runs better in the humid weather."

"What about all my shit? It was in the cab."

Darla refused to look him in the eye, it had boiled his blood something awful. "If this is what you're referring to, it's right over here." She indicated a pile of dusty clothes, interspersed with a couple of flannels, a pair of sunglasses, a nudie deck of playing cards, a prehistoric copper Zippo lighter and a box of old toothpicks with a faded price tag of thirty-three cents still on it.

Charlie felt as if he were in a daze, but still conscious enough to want nothing more than to exit the room. If Hal had actually been there, and it would've been rare to see him that late at night, he might not have been in such a hurry. They probably would've shot the shit for an hour even, before Charlie would hand over his pre-trip report and be on his merry way.

He scooped up his belongings from the old five and started to walk out.

Darla snapped her stubby fingers together behind him, "Mr. Coldbrick, I still need those keys for the five."

Once outside again, Charlie hurriedly lit another Red. He paused for a moment to let a momentary breeze sweep across him, he was already pouring sweat, and he usually only did that near state lines. Never could he figure it out. One day he finally chalked it up to the fact that a chicken coop was always on the other side, packed full of DOT bears – waiting for him.

They were always there. In that passing, fleeting glimpse when Charlie would roll by them, they somehow were always wearing their invisible, x-ray goggles; able to see every molecule of rust on a cracked kingpin, or a bent steering axle. Or that your comic book is missing a line between six and ten, or even a tire that is inflated two psi's under the legal limit.

The smug smirks that would develop on their faces when they found an infraction was enough for Charlie to want to rip their heads off and shit down their necks. Worst of all, they got to hide behind a seemingly righteous cause, one that anybody, including Charlie, would be crazy to argue with: safety.

Safe or not, Charlie understood that DOTS were quite possibly the lowest form of human life. They're the bacteria that feed on disease, which is why no self respecting truck driver should ever show them an inkling of civility.

And here I am, Charlie thought. *Probably gonna grind the hellfire outta those gears before I even make it to Nebraska. Then once I reach the first station on the other side, they'll be able to bend me over nice and proper.*

But what does a whole mess of fines and lost time concern a cunt like Darla for? When bitches like that take hold of the reigns, they don't break you in. They use shock and awe. They gotta hit you with something right away, letting you know who's in charge. Especially a dyke like her, Charlie thought. *She really thinks she has something to prove to a guy like me.* So she vindictively stuck him with the ten, knowing full well that Charlie had driven nothing but the five for the past several years.

"Jesus Christ," he muttered through his sour breath, thinking about having to work for that woman. He tossed his Red over the railing and sauntered down the steps. Suddenly, Charlie had lost a decent amount of respect for his company. How could the powers-that-be pluck out a decent man like Hal and plug the hole with a filthy rag like Darla. However, it wasn't the first time the world had confused and disappointed him – not by a long shot. And he whole-heartedly doubted that it would be the last.

He glanced over at the ten speed which seemed to glare back at him behind its faded red paint. Its filthy, stained headlights. He was trying to remember the last time anyone had that fucker inspected. The last time he drove a ten was when the five badly needed a retarder replaced. That was eight years ago, and only to Cheyenne, Wyoming.

After he got his stuff packed into the cab, he remembered the papers. He tore them out of their manila envelope and glared at two sections: *Shipment ordered by:* and *Tractor Number:* Both were blank. But there was almost a hint of black ink behind "tractor number," almost as if someone had used white-out.

Why in the hell ain't I notice this last week when I opened it?

Charlie couldn't tell for sure. He had seen them so often before, they all seemed to blur together. He may have seen "Hal" in his mind, but in reality it was blank. But TEMPE sure read loud and clear.

After thoroughly inspecting the ten and checking the air in the brakelines, Charlie groaned up the steps once again. He didn't want to see his new boss again. Fate smiled upon him a bit, because when he went to turn the knob, he felt enough resistance to learn it was locked. Darla, the dyke, had gone home.

He shoved the pre-trip through the mail slot and took off awkwardly in the ten, kicking up a dust bowl large enough to create a shadow on a football stadium. He stopped only briefly to pick up the trailer in Lennox, then he was on his way. He lunged and lurched, grinding the gears all the way, just like he anticipated. Then he was back on I-29 again, heading south.

As the whiny sound of eighteen wheels grazing the asphalt below filled him, he briefly wondered how long it would be until he scratched his face again.

<u>3</u>

"Daydreams: This used to be my Playground"

Once he crossed that state line into Iowa, Charlie was able to breathe a bit easier. He didn't ever want to go back, not with that sour succubus running things. As he listened to the garbled banter on Sesame Street, channel 19, he lit up a Red and briefly entertained the notion of quitting. After the load in Tempe, he would drive right back to Benson Road and tell that hag exactly what he thought of her and her kind. He grinned, exposing his rotting epidermis to the last of the Dakota wind when he pictured how they would beg him to stay.

And why wouldn't they? He had given them his life and all he received in return was grief. Grief, and warning after warning; threat after threat. When and if the day came he finally would receive his gold watch, Charlie only pictured a cheap imitation. Copper at best. Just like his long lasting fire breathing friend that they savagely ripped from the five. The trusty old Zippo he bought in Reno, Nevada in '76.

Please Charlie... we neeeeed you, they would bellow.

Charlie hawked another one up and giggled for a couple of reasons. One, because their cries would fall on deaf, chilly, unforgiving ears, if that day were to come. And two, because some trucker on Sesame Street from Sioux City was telling an amusing joke involving a woman with saddlebags trying to ride coach on an airplane.

When Charlie reached Sergeant Bluff, he groaned at the sight of an approaching weigh station. Fate smiled upon him again when those shiny white letters pulsated in seemingly midair along side the highway when his headlamps breached them, *STATION CLOSED*. He was happy. For the first time on this trip something had gone his way. He was so happy that he pulled right up that ramp, dummied up and joined the half dozen other wagons.

As he placed his boots in the back of the cab, sucking on a Red, trying not to scratch his arid face, he realized he *had* been out of service for a while. He remembered thinking only hours earlier that he would be in Colorado by morning. He hadn't even made Nebraska yet. He was still thinking too much like the old days. Back when the landscape was his playground. Back then, he'd drive twelve…thirteen hours without batting an eye. Now, if he drove anything over four, they'd squeeze his tit harder than an IRS agent giving an audit.

Charlie touched his face and briefly thought that his curse was spreading to his brain and had somehow warped his sense of time. But then he quickly dismissed it. "They're counting on me," he gunned hard on his stick. "I ain't gonna let 'em down just yet."

Charlie felt better than he had expected when he awoke to a mostly cloudy sky with hints of sprinkles misting his windshield. Two things were apparent as he opened his half glued eyes. The thing on his face that itched so mercilessly had gotten worse (and he didn't have to look in the mirror to know that). A white-hot stinging sensation erupted from it the moment he regained consciousness in the bunk of the cab. It felt to Charlie like someone had come along during the night and grinded six layers of his skin apart, and now they were all mixed up in little strands, twisting together and impossible to untangle. He felt the need to wash up, but the pain made him ponder it longer than normal. On a windy day in the Great Plains, a guy can step out into the open air at any time and get a face full of soot and earth.

The other thing that occurred to Charlie was that he was going to have to drive the ten again. He hated it. Not just because it had so many gears he had only been acquainted with too many years ago, but also because of the stink that wafted through it when he awoke. He understood, sure, that he was partly to blame. But when old Hal was running things, this monster was driven by more truckers than the town whore with no teeth. It was the village bicycle of *Pioneer Trucking Inc.*

He stepped out into the Iowa morning, the air was a bit crisp for August. But he knew it would only be a matter of time before that hot Grand Island sun would return and boil the tar on the highway. After a brief trip to the head, Charlie performed a half assed inspection of the red monster, filled in the lines of his comic book clumsily, and hit the road toward Omaha.

He had better luck shifting, he developed a certain rhythm with the truck that he thought may never have surfaced. Things were looking up, he was able to drive his four hours peacefully. Bantering with passing rigmasters on Sesame Street, smoking Reds, and oogling at some of the finest young maidens that Iowa had to offer. They mostly passed him in the hammer lane, their cars full to the brim with useless trinkets. Back to fall semester at the University of Nebraska or Missouri or wherever.

In that time he had only itched three times and it only bled once. Even the stinging sensation waned. Once I-29 was surrounded by more prairie land, he rolled down his window and let the cool wind brush against his sweaty face.

Everything was going fine, then he reached Council Bluffs and had to stop at a station, a DOT interment camp. Contrary to his uneventful morning, the lot was clusterfucked.

The place was one giant headache, cars backfiring sickly, toxic smells that caused Charlie's stomach to roundabout. Kids were screaming while their mothers smiled and held their husband's hands. The whole thing seemed like an intrusion. So many four wheelers were parked in the overflow that the half dozen rigs had to form a single line to be weighed. And worse still, they were inspecting everyone.

A hard, heavy lump formed instantly in Charlie's throat, he quickly lit a Red to neutralize it. *This fuckin' truck*, he thought spastically. *They're going to bend me over nice and proper.*

"I need this," Charlie moaned to himself. "I need this like I need a hole in my pocket on payday."

<u>4</u>

"The Red Wicked Witch of Council Bluffs"

As the line slowly meandered to just three rigs in front of him, the four wheelers rudely tried to barge their way through. It was as if Charlie and his fellow eighteen wheeled chariots were invisible. As if these prides were the kings and queens of the highway. Charlie flipped the bird to a woman in her thirties who nearly grazed his front bumper with her outrageously large *Sport Utility Vehicle*. Her husband glared out from the other side, but that was all he could do. She was yelling something at him as she sped down the onramp at a conservative 2 miles per gallon.

Charlie quickly tried to forget about the rotten gifts he would like to bestow upon those road hogs, for his turn was next.

He rolled smoothly up to the scale without lurching the tractor at all. These dogs would even scold you on improper braking if they're in a really bad mood. Charlie wasn't about to give them a thing that could be pinned on him. He just wanted to get through the mess and back out to his playground.

The DOT inspector was an Indian woman in her thirties, her hate-filled, ugly eyes looked as red as the rocks on Mars. She had a slithery tongue that refused to sit still in her awkward mouth, when she spoke she sounded like a transvestite that went a little heavy on the hormone shots.

"I need to see your papers."

Charlie handed them over, rolling his eyes and flicking his cigarette without saying a word.

She looked them over carefully, for the briefest of moments Charlie thought her fiery eyes would burn pinholes right through the crumpled sheets and for a grand finale the stapled documents would erupt in spontaneous combustion. Meanwhile, her lackeys circled the red monster in haphazard, jerky movements for what seemed like forever. The woman glanced up from the papers at Charlie, she tried to look right through him. He quickly turned away as if he'd been staring at the sun. *She ain't gonna pull no injun tricks on me*, he thought quietly to himself.

When he glanced out the corner of his eye she was gone, circling the monster with the others. A droplet of sweat rolled onto Charlie's face, stinging it like a snakebite. He bit his lip until it bled to keep from screaming. He was being tested, and it was a pass/fail kind of deal.

The DOT witch had appeared just as suddenly as she left. "What are you hauling, sir?"

"As far as I know, they're pallets of dry noodles from *Barilla*." *That's good*, he thought, *don't say anymore than you have to. Don't give this sorceress an inch to work with.*

"Well, you have the wrong placard displayed," she grumbled, pointing over her shoulder. And sure enough, this icy bitch was as power-hungry as the rest of them. Out came the little pad that indicated he was going to have to open his checkbook after all.

Charlie sighed and tried to bite his tongue, but it was too late. "What the fuck is it displaying, then?"

She looked up and glared at him, "Don't push it, buddy," her genderless voice boomed. "It said you were carrying an oxidizer. I need you're A-card and any endorsements. I also need your log book. While I'm doing that, why don't you go change that placard?"

Charlie pushed all the rage he had at his fingertips, deep down into his stomach until it felt as heavy as a moon-rock. He dug out his comic and license from the cab and practically threw it at her. No sense in being nice anymore. She was going to give it

nice and proper

to him no matter what.

The fire breathing whore. Gist a couple of generations removed from red, little men wearing feathers, chanting and dancing around a fire like a bunch of loonies. She ain't even going to break me in first.

She glared at him as he passed her, each now really getting a good look at the other. Quickly her eyes darted back down to the hefty fine she was no doubt writing him, the fire giving way to a flushed, almost remorseful look.

Charlie ambled past her, spat and fumed at the placard. That thin piece of metal would soon cost him an arm and a leg. On display was the top of a match head, a solid orange on top and bright electric blue in the middle of the flame. Printed across it in large, looming letters was the word: OXIDIZER, and a decimal on the bottom, 5.1.

She probably changed it, Charlie thought to himself.

Forcefully, he turned the metal latches that held the card in place and began flipping through: Dangerous, Poison, Non-Flammable Gas, Corrosive, until finally he came upon the blank one. He slammed it open and the razor, slim, perturbing metal put a slice the size of a small paper clip in his index finger. He let out a whisper-cry, but no more. Awkwardly, he latched the placard into place with his left hand and shook his finger at the ground.

Blood flew from his digit in sticky forming strings, like snot from a raggedy Kleenex. But it was amazing how quickly he clotted, the thick protruding droplets gave way to a regular, controlled flow. Truth be told, Charlie was more concerned with his vicious, throbbing face, which came off in yellow crusts when he picked at it.

He rung around the backside of his trailer, faintly giving the stink-eye to the other DOT bears as he took care of the other placard. "TIE-ROD-BENT-ON-INSIDE-WHEEL-FRONT!" one of them shouted hoarsely. At that moment, all the blood seemed to flow out of Charlie's hand from the inside. It was like a vacuum, it flew warp-speed to the inside of his ears. He could hear whooshing ten times louder than Niagara Falls. For a moment, his truck wasn't there at all. He saw a great field of red. Embedded in the middle of it was the injun woman's slightly bemused smirk as she wrote the infraction down on her pad.

Charlie swallowed hard again and calmly yelled, "The fuck it is, I had all this inspected thoroughly before I left Sioux Falls."

The guy looked up, he was at least ten years younger and ten times fitter than Charlie, he had a push-broom mustache and tattoos seeping out the sleeves of his shirt. Charlie snapped his mouth shut again, he didn't want to take it out on a hard working man who happened to be in the wrong profession. He was saving most of his fire for the injun.

Aggravated to no end, he scratched at his face until he realized he had grease mixed with blood embedded under his fingernails. He knew at any moment that sharp, lily pain would return to wreak havoc on his nerves. But first he had to go get it *nice and proper*.

He came face to face with the DOT ice queen at the hood of the red monster. He backed a few steps away as she did the same, carefully avoiding his face. She looked off to the side of him as she handed back the license and comic book. "These check out, but I'm going to have to get that tie rod fixed. It's at a critical point…and if you're headed for Tempe – then I have no choice. Out of service, twenty-four hours."

Charlie stared at her with all the loathing he had at his disposal. "Look at me and say it," his voice shuddered.

She glanced hotly and met his stare. She *was* trying to be respectful before, but she was not afraid of him. She was the ice princess that Charlie had her pegged for. "You heard me just fine. This act ain't gonna help you neither. We'll fix the tie rod and bill the appropriate people, but we're fining you $850."

At that moment, something in Charlie's head screamed like a tea kettle and a new born baby combined. In a cartoon, the smoke whizzing out of his ears would be enough to cover an entire square mile of the highway.

He opened his mouth to call her a *bitch*, but she continued before he could. "It's quite generous – considering. And since I'm feeling so generous this afternoon, we're gonna grease your fifth wheel at no extra charge. It needs it. I heard you say that this was inspected before you left –

well – the sticker is three months expired. We'll have to bill your company for that too. Take it around the station and fill out this report – sign it at the bottom." She shoved the papers into his arms and frantically pointed where he needed to go.

Before he could give any response, she was pointing to the next truck in line, a bullhauler. Charlie glared at her, wanting to spew his hate in every direction. Not only did she do him *nice and proper*, but she wanted him to thank her. So many obscenities and vulgarities came to his mind at once that they all became gridlocked in his throat, much like the clusterfucked lot he stood in. To his own self disgust, he obeyed her and climbed in his truck without saying a word. He looked down at his index finger, he was putting so much pressure on his hand from making a fist that the blood flowed more gingerly. He thought if he squeezed hard enough he just might be able to shoot out a bone fragment like a cannonball. And he knew right then and there where he would aim his crosshairs.

He slammed the steering wheel of the ten and cruelly smashed into first gear. He drove around the building like he was told and followed the finger puppets of another DOT dog pointing him toward a garage stall. He filled out the 'out of service' report and heaved it at him. He went inside the station, fisted a quarter through a pay phone and dialed Darla, the dyke.

Everything was going so fast that the situation swirled in and around his head. For the first time in years, Charlie felt like he had to vomit rage from every orifice.

When he heard her shrill voice on the other end of the line he quickly slammed the receiver down, loud enough to at least give her a headache. Almost tripping over himself, he marched outside and up to the scale where the Indian woman was conversing with the driver of the bullhauler.

Before she could stop him, he got it out, "I just want to know one thing. What's a dirty, red puss like you working for the goddamn DOT fer? What'samatter? Fucking Iowa not cutting the Sioux-eee enough checks? Did fucking over the card player get old? I'll tell you one thing you snake riding, fire worshipping, peyote eating, white man scalping bitch. You ain't never gonna bring me DOWN! NEVER!! Cause you NEED me! You NEED all of us!" Charlie panted and wheezed, he felt like he was back. He had done this sort of thing all the time before, which is why the powers-that-be were always riding him. He didn't even care if this one would cost him his job *and* gold watch. "If you were a man I would punch your goddamn lights out and use them to mark your grave!"

One of her DOT assistants noticed the tirade Charlie was going off on and made a step toward them. But she calmly put her hand up, stopping him in his tracks. She stepped toward Charlie and leaned in, "If I were a man, you wouldn't live to see another station. If you don't get outta my sight in two seconds, I'm pulling your license and shutting down your company."

Charlie stormed toward the direction of town in the middle of her sentence, he wasn't going to listen to another word. There was only one thing he needed, and he needed it more than life itself.

<u>5</u>

"Drowning in the Seventh Sea"

Like a volcano prepared to erupt, he stormed down the road in large, awkward paces. His bulky build heaved in the wind as he reached in his pocket to fish out a Red.

Oops, left em' in the truck, old buddy.

Quickening his erroneous pace, he hawked one up and spat instead. It sizzled under the tyranny of the sun when it hit the pavement. But it may have been because Charlie's fury was still sending blood-filled smoke signals. He worked up a sweat rather quickly, his slick fingers managed to pull out a bandana from his back pocket and he wiped fiercely at his forehead. Then, maybe to get it all out, he dabbed lightly at his face.

The screams were hard and blood curdling. But the sound of Charlie putting out airs was soon drowned out by a more robust, familiar sound. A rough and ragged diesel engine was approaching him from behind.

The driver of the bullhauler gave Charlie a ride to the next exit, suburban Council Bluffs, or as suburban as it could get for Iowa. He was a nice young kid, only in his fourth year driving. He didn't like Charlie, that much was evident, anyone in their right mind who'd witnessed the scene back at the scales wouldn't have. Plus, he noticed as Charlie was climbing in that he spat at the cattle and cackled, "See you boys at McDonald's next month." But he was one of those ignorant, young souls that still fully endorsed the dreaded *trucker code*.

Young, dumb and full of come, Charlie reminisced of his early days driving truck on the way into town. The kid was nice enough to find a service station to drop him off at. Calmer, Charlie shook his hand and thanked him kindly as he dropped himself out of the cab. But he secretly was more pleasant because he noticed a tavern across the road called *The Leatherneck*.

After buying some smokes at the service station, he ventured in and took a post near the end by the taps. It was a dark bar, which suited Charlie just fine. The only light that spilled in was between the blinds and it was a filtered, smoky light at that. Charlie ordered his usual seven-seven and lit a Red as he sipped. Not too much clientele in these types of places in the middle of the afternoon. An old farmer who kept glancing at his dog tied to a chair in the corner, and a younger, smaller guy at a table in a clip-on suit and tie who looked down on his luck.

On his second seven-seven, Charlie grumbled to himself about the bartender staring at (his face) him strangely and pulled his crumpled, carbon copy of the 'Out of Service' report from his jean jacket. He pulled the Red from his mouth, stubbed it out, and replaced it with a toothpick. Charlie studied the report in the dim light until he found what he was looking for. It stated that he couldn't drive his rig any further until 2:30 PM CDT the next day. Even though his juices were a bit scarce from the dusty surroundings, Charlie managed to spit on the report and set fire to it with his Zippo, drawing more strange looks from the bartender and farmer. The man at the table was suddenly too concerned with a crossword he had pulled from his briefcase.

The more Charlie examined the situation internally, the more his fists bent up in odd, infrequent jerks. The sound of his blood beginning to boil between his ears soon followed, so he started to grind his teeth to counteract it.

He sat at his perch, drinking the seven-seven's (he lost count after number eight), and smoked all the Reds he could muster. Of course the time went fast, always does when you tip a few. Charlie tipped his share, all the while becoming more and more furious. Every little thing set him off inside. The stares, the whispers between the bartenders when it was shift change, the way the guy in back playing pool laughed obnoxiously, the way his face seared and itched.

But still, Charlie did nothing about any of it. Instead of looking for a reasonable motel for the night, instead of concocting a plan to be back at the scales at exactly 2:30 PM the next day, he merely sat stewing, sipping the sour seven-seven bitterly between his teeth.

<u>6</u>

"The Hit Heard Round the Leatherneck"

By the time the nine to fiver's started to roll in, the place was becoming a bit more lively. However, Charlie was too drunk to notice. By his skewed calculation, he should have been halfway into Colorado. But there he was, sitting in some floozy drunk tank in Council Bluffs, waiting to cross the border into Nebraska. It had been a rotten way to start a trip, which had been cursed from the start by Darla.

Now the injun bitch, he thought, grimacing. *Always in the way of progress.*

A clatter to Charlie's left sounded off in the bar when a rough looking guy in his forties stepped in and stared hard. He was wearing a greased up tank T-shirt and had a helmet of some kind under his oily armpit. Anyone who hadn't known him already might have guessed he was in construction, or possibly a miner. Had Charlie been more lucid, it may have reminded him of one of those scenes in movies where a badass walks in, the music stops and everyone turns to look. Only this badass was real. But like in the movies, he had two equally greasy, goofy looking guys with him. Each with his own jagged sense of reality and crooked looking face.

Charlie hardly noticed any of this, they were mere cliff notes compared to the rest of the information sifting through his mind. Nevertheless, the man had some sort of status among the regular patrons, because they seemed to avoid looking at him. Much in the way most of them avoided looking at Charlie if they had happened to glance at his face earlier that night.

It didn't take the badass and his goons long to single out the stranger. Some kind of strange turn of luck found the seats near Charlie empty. The badass approached and stared at him with a deep, intruding glance. He stared for a full three minutes before Charlie even noticed. But at that point, he was too liquored up to care, he just sat in the position he'd been all day (only getting up four times to piss) and puffed away on his Red. One thing the sauce did for Charlie, it mellowed him out some. He was still capable of deep-seeded, violent anger himself when he was half in the bag, it's just that he wasn't goaded as easily. But with the kind of day Charlie had had, it was a miracle he held off as long as he did.

"JES-USSS KRAHIST, MAN. SOMEONE TAKE A SHIIIT ON YER FACE?" the badass ran out of patience, waiting for Charlie to ask why he was staring at him. "GIT MIXED UP WITH DA WROONG HOOKER? GODDAMN, I CAN SEE THEM CAL-LIH-FLOWRA THINGS ALREADY STARTIN' TO SPROUT!"

Charlie only made out half of what he was saying, he simply burped out a puff of smoke in the posse's direction.

The smile on the badass' face didn't completely cloud over, but still waned a bit. The new bartender, a heavy-set, ex-con looking guy with tattoos running up and down his arms waddled over to the badass with a shot of brown liquor. To emphasize his point even more, the badass downed the shot without changing his face or even looking away from Charlie. "Another one," he commanded the bartender.

"You can have another two on the house if promise you won't leave here tonight in handcuffs or a stretcher," the bartender grumbled in a gruff voice.

"I promise you," he smiled harder at Charlie, "*I* won't be leavin' on no stretcher."

"Ain't nobody leaving on a stretcher," he sealed their agreement by pouring the shots, one for each of his associates as well.

It slowly began to sink in for Charlie that the words the man spoke were fightin'. His battered fingers nimbly touched the buck knife through the pocket of his jeans, he did it slyly, like he wasn't moving at all – only swaying in drunken circles. The brief heart murmur he felt as the badass stared on was actually sobering him up, at least enough to put a dent in the guy's chiseled face. Enough to make it look worse than his own.

It had been a while, but Charlie was silently preparing himself for one last brawl, he didn't think he'd ever be in the situation again. But Lord knows he had seen his share in the past. Almost lost his job over a couple of them, but Hal was always there to smooth things over. It looked like the chance to roll those same pair of die was there for the taking, only Darla would take the ample opportunity to make an example of him.

T.S., Charlie thought, *this is better than any gold watch, anyhow.*

But no way was he going to start it, Charlie knew that much for sure. He would have a better chance of wriggling out of the situation later if it looked like self-defense. The ball was in the badass' court. After all, Charlie wouldn't have minded leaving town without any more trouble. So the badass would have to play white and make the first move.

It was obvious to anyone who had been watching the situation unfold that the badass wasn't nearly as systematic as Charlie was. Before long, he was pushing him, lightly at first, but then faster and faster. Hard enough to make Charlie's stool rock back and forth. Several patrons looked on in their own glazed amusement. "YOU LOOK AT ME WHEN I TALK TO YOU! YOU REDNECK ASSHOLE!"

Charlie was about to make his move, but light shoving wasn't enough. It turned out he was able to hold out for a bit longer. Also, a euphoric sense of amusement was shading him because of how pissed the badass was getting when Charlie refused to acknowledge him.

"YOU CAL-LIH-FLOWR-ING FAGGOT!"

As the badass' voice grew more shrill, more and more patrons were turning their heads, some muttering *pussy* under their breath about Charlie. But to Charlie, that only made the payoff that much better. To exceed expectations to an exponential degree.

"YA FUCKIN' LEPER!"

He had done it this way often before, not only to give the crowd an unexpected twist, but also the other fighter. In fact, Charlie can only think of one time when he actually started the fight.

"YOU DON'T BELON' AT THE LEATHERNECK, BOY. YOU BELON' IN A PLASTIC BUBBLE!"

It was in San Francisco, a couple of decades ago. He walked into a bar on Mission Street looking for some action, but found the wrong kind. When some guy cupped Charlie's nuts in his hand, he nearly beat him half to death. Back in those days, even in a liberal city as Frisco, he only got a weekend in San Francisco County jail and a $300 fine.

"YOU LOOK AT ME WHEN I TALK TO YOU YOU FUCKIN' FREAK!"

By the time he got out, he was five days late on his load. This was a time in trucking before the DOT started setting regulations. Unfair demands on drivers, unstable unions, guys staying up three, sometimes four days straight to make a load.

"YOU FAT FUCKIN' SLOB! I'M GONNA CLOCK YOU ONE!"

All those years on the road, all the places he'd been, the friends he had made and lost. All the fights, brawls and scuffles he had partaken. Charlie Coldbrick had never met anyone so hell-bent on duking it out before. He finally looked over at the badass, his eyes were in a frenzy, his brow was sprinkled with sweat and his lower lip quivered a bit. The man probably felt Charlie had insulted him in the worst way by not opening his mouth to answer him.

"What's your name?" the badass asked in a gentler tone.

"Charlie Coldbrick."

"CHARLIE GOLD-BRICK! THAT'S A FUCKIN' HOOT AND A HOLLER, AIN'T IT? WELL NOW, I'S BEGINNIN' TO THINK YOU WERE ONE OF THEM DEAF-FUCKIN'-MUTES!"

"Well, it turns out I'm not after all."

"FUCK YOU!"

"No thanks," Charlie knew his kind and he felt for certain that would do it nicely.

It did, because Charlie was too busy blinking, but he felt the sharp pain on his face double. If the searing was white hot before, it was blinding now. But what difference did any of that make any longer? The badass had clocked him one as promised. It sobered him up even more.

Charlie bent down, doubled over, he let a tiny whining sound escape from his lips. This made the badass, his cronies and several of the patrons laugh an almost pitiful wheeze. When the badass turned halfway around to the crowd, Charlie struck. He made contact with the side of his face, for the first time in his life, feeling teeth loosen beneath his knuckles.

The badass responded with a shriek and it was on. He grabbed the nearest bottle at his disposal, which turned out to be half full of *Red Dog* and smashed it to smithereens. He aimed it at Charlie, but that was all he could muster. Charlie gave him a full-throttled, perfectly timed kick in the abdomen. The badass dropped to a knee, wheezing and gasping, as if the oxygen supply on earth was about to run out at any moment. He dropped the half broken bottle and it shattered into more pieces.

One of his minions smashed Charlie on the side of his face, the side that was already hurting. The blinding pain almost blacked him out momentarily, but he was able to stay on his feet and elbow the guy in the neck. He dropped easily to the floor and landed on his ass. His face turned so red that it almost reminded Charlie of a toddler falling down and was seconds away from wailing his head off.

The other guy stared at Charlie, as the badass slowly rose off his wounded knee. Charlie wasn't sure if he was sizing him up still, or if he was scared to attack – it could've been both. The badass wailed indistinguishable screams and pounced at Charlie who had to do nothing more but step out of the way. The badass was so blind with blank rage that he ran another ten feet before he stopped and turned around. That was when his other second-in-command decided to try and put Charlie in a choke hold. The guy was strong, but Charlie was still stronger. All those years of getting paid cash to lump many of his own trailers had paid off. He wasn't strong enough (or the guy wasn't light enough) to flip him over his body the way they do in the movies, but Charlie drove his head backwards and he heard himself break the guy's nose.

He began screaming and covered his face like a child watching a scary movie. Blood spurted from between his fingers before he collapsed to the ground. That made Charlie real sick to his stomach, these three wanting so badly to fight him and following their words up with such disgusting, cowardly actions. The scene of the man bent over on the ground even stopped the badass in his tracks and caused him to wrinkle his nose.

The screaming was so bad that it felt like a tea kettle was whistling between Charlie's ears, to him it sounded worse than a rabbit being eaten alive.

"SHUT UUUPPP!" Charlie screamed hoarsely at him.

The wailing got worse and more high pitched, more blood poured between the man's fingers. The scene had gotten ugly, some patrons had begun to stand, some simply turned away in revulsion. The ex-con looking bartender looked like he was about to make a move to break it up. But Charlie noticed none of this, he couldn't have continued until the screaming ceased. It felt like his guts were about to explode.

"SHUT THE FUCK UP!!!" he yelled at the bawling man again.

But the man didn't stop, he only carried on louder and sharper. So Charlie grabbed his hands and put them behind his back like he had a pair of handcuffs. With one of his tree trunk arms he was able to hold both of them while he took his other palm and mashed the guy's face into the floor full of broken glass. Charlie, on the verge of passing out, made sure to twist the guy's face into the shards to stop the siren sound of his voice.

It worked, but by the time Charlie realized the badass was charging in at him, it was too late. He felt, skinny, hairy knuckles imbed in almost slow motion into his larynx. It was as if Charlie's windpipe was as thin as a strand of hair and someone had taken a pair of scissors and went 'SNIP'. The world turned black and faded into blue before his eyes. He felt his leg stumble backwards, but he didn't fall over. The badass made another move to finish him off, but somehow Charlie's reflexes responded. He grabbed him by his hair and flung him head-on into the jukebox with more strength than anyone who isn't able to breathe should be capable of.

The badass landed in a pile of broken glass, wood splinters, shards of light bulbs and a heap of broken CCR and Waylon Jennings records. Just then, he heard a handset bounce off a cradle as the bartender was picking up the phone to call the bears. Charlie grasped at his neck and twisted to try and straighten the windpipe. He was able to cough, but it came out in a spat of blood. He gagged and did it again. When he inhaled on the third try he felt the cool wind of fresh oxygen burn against the blood pooling in his throat.

That will have to be enough for now, he thought. He collected his pack of Reds from the bartop, which inexplicably remained in their spot during the melee and high-tailed it out of the *Leatherneck*.

Once outside and over the initial shock that it was dark out and he was in a town he didn't know – he ran. Hobbled was more like it. As much as Charlie would've liked to think otherwise, he wasn't a young pup anymore. That scene in the *Leatherneck* had truly hurt him more than he realized. He was sure in that hazy moment that he would feel it the next day.

As the sweat rolled down his face, he kept on running. He ran until he could no longer see any solid objects around him. He ran until his guts burst and his head combusted. He ran straight into oblivion – then he collapsed to the ground.

<u>7</u>

"Something in the Air"

This case was interesting to beat the band. Detectives Aspen and Tucker couldn't have been more enthralled in what they were involved with. It was terribly embarrassing the way it was the talk of the County Crime Division, as well as a hit in local papers such as *The Silver Belt* and *Payson Roundup*. They even had a fed come out a few days after they had stumbled upon the scene to review the file they had built so far.

In a strange sort of way, it strengthened their relationship too. They began calling one another at home to discuss the in's and out's and exploring every possible path the case could stray.

But it certainly hadn't done their family lives any good. Cynthia Aspen had kicked her husband out of bed on three separate occasions since he and Tucker found Charlie for reading and re-reading the case notes too vigorously late at night. Martha Tucker wept uncontrollably when her other half had failed to pick up the antibiotic for their sick five year old, Tanya, one night at the local pharmacy.

They were both well aware of the common cliché: two detectives sweating over a case that never reveals itself, neglecting their families, being verbally roughhoused by the chief for not using proper procedure. It had TV movie of the week written all over it. But like all flavors of the month, the general public soon began to lose interest.

Still, it was one of the strangest cases that either had ever been involved with. And for them, it was far too intoxicating to focus on anything otherwise. The reason it lit such a fire was the fact that they were no closer to obtaining the next big break. The last one they had was when they found Charlie's wallet in the cab that momentous day in the desert.

On September 30th, they were both secretly sure that the big piece was about to fall into their lap. It had been six days since their fruitful discovery. Six days since the only witness to the scene had been admitted to *Good Samaritan*, recovering from a nasty car accident. Six days before they were eventually given clearance by the Chief hospital admin doctor to interview the witness. It was a day they were both panting for, and on September 30th that day had finally arrived.

The morning nurse was frumpy, she walked in awkward paces as Aspen and Tucker followed closely behind her. She led them down endless, sprawling, bright-white corridors that smelled of bleach and were serenaded by the sounds of oxygen tubes and heart monitors. Instinctively, Aspen held his crotch until the latest twinge of pain had passed.

Tucker noticed instantly, he thought of his partner like a child who had drank too much chocolate milk and had no inhibitions about dancing around in a circle. He even once shared this observation with him on one of the nights they had discussed the case. He had developed, over the last six days, a kind of reverent sympathy for Aspen. It suddenly struck him when he stopped by his house and watched him interact with his son Bailey a couple of nights before. They had never regretted each other using that type of subjective humanity before.

And they both felt it, even if they hadn't openly talked about it. The feeling was there – surrounding them as they hammered away at the peculiar details of the case.

Tucker leaned in on his partner as they followed the dowdy nurse, "You know, as long as we're here, maybe you should get that checked out."

"What are you talking about?" Aspen asked, pretending to be taken aback.

"You don't have to play coy with me. I know you're hurtin'."

This time it was Aspen who grinned a bit, despite the urinary pain. "You know, Tuck, you're starting to sound like my wife." The grin on his face grew three sizes. It was followed by a couple of stifled laughs that escaped from his lips.

Then, as if planned all along, laughter exploded from the two detectives. The nurse slowed her waddle to turn around and scowl at them, as if questioning their ethics and professionalism. Her reaction and the stress of working over the case for the last six days and six nights only caused them to laugh harder. Their laughter echoed through the hollow halls of *Good Samaritan*. They didn't care. They needed an icebreaker before they got down to business. Besides, they had shared one other comradery between them since the Coldbrick case began to unfold – both of their wives were furious at them over it.

After what seemed like another mile walked through the dazzling, glossy maze of the hospital, the nurse finally stopped outside a room like all the others. The blank, colored plaques above the door were all flush with the wall except the yellow one, which was pointing outward, indicating the room was being occupied by a patient. "Gentleman, this is the young lady's room." She hesitated before she continued, "Now remember what Doctor Schwartz discussed with you. Her condition is stable for now, but she's on a lot of pain medication, so go easy with the questions. I'll come back in a while to see how you're doing."

"Thank you…" Tucker glanced at her ID tag, "Edna."

She smiled skeptically and turned around quickly as she toddled off to the nurses' station. Her hips thrusted in diagonal motions as she appeared to be walking sideways, but still somehow managed to move forward.

"Okay?" Aspen asked his partner, quickly becoming anxious to keep their winning streak alive.

"Okay." Tucker replied with more finality.

Their loafers squeaked as they entered the room. A bright yellow wet floor sign stood on its post a few feet away, and a janitor mopping an already pristine floor worked about ten feet farther. The room was littered with brightly colored cards and balloons. Gift baskets and other trinkets had been piled on the bed where the roommate would usually sleep. However, this patient was involved with something a bit more public than most, so the hospital had opted to allow Abby to room alone.

The sun winked through the blinds casting a light on her sleeping eyes as they gyrated from the air conditioning vent a few feet above. Otherwise, the rest of the room remained dim and static. Aspen noticed a few pictures standing erect on a shelf above her bed, assuming it was of her family so she wouldn't get lonely. He suddenly had a flash back to when his little boy had to get his tonsils removed, and what it was like staying up with him the night before, writhing in his four year old pain. But he quickly dismissed the feeling, there was business to attend to.

Tucker slowly and meticulously opened the shades, allowing the pleasant morning light to swallow the room.

Abby stirred and opened her eyes a quarter of the way. She was fifteen with pleasant yellow hair, and a volleyball physique.

Tucker noticed she was tall, but still looked very young, like her body was a cast of what she'll look like as an adult, but she was still in the process of growing into it. "Hello Abby," he said in his gravely no-nonsense voice.

"Hi," she said sitting up, looking a bit anxious, yet somehow not surprised to see them.

"I'm detective Tucker, and this is my partner Aspen. We've been waiting to chat with you about what happened last week. We just want to ask you a few questions, nothing prolonged. Are you feeling up to that?"

"Yeah, okay," a sigh escaped her lips after a few moments.

"We spoke to your Mom briefly on the phone a few days ago. She did tell you we were coming, didn't she?"

"She told me someone would come and ask me questions. So you guys are like – police?"

"Well, we work for the Gila County Crime Division as investigators. We are just trying to figure out what happened with the accident and with you and if we need to pursue anything further. But first we want to establish the facts. I'll tell you what we've learned and maybe you can tell us if we have anything wrong. Sound okay?"

"You're going to ask me about Charlie, aren't you?"

The newly invigorated partners exchanged a quick glance. Something seemed wrong. The air of confidence they walked in with appeared to have vanished somehow. The atmosphere had shifted in some way. It wasn't anything Abby had said or done, nothing tangible was even at fault. It was just something in the air.

"Well, eventually we will, but we need to ask some other things first," Aspen piped in. "We uh – do you want anything before we begin? A glass of water or something?"

"No thank you."

"Well Abby, we have quite a little mystery on our hands here and we were hoping that you could help us out with it," Tucker explained, retaking control of the reigns that steered the conversation.

It was fine with Aspen, his infection began to twinge all over again. He was fine with taking notes while his partner went to the plate.

"He saved me, you know," her battered voice squeaked matter of factly. She had probably screamed her voice hoarse for help in the hours following the accident.

"We can get to that in a minute. First of all, when we talked to your Mom, she told us that you didn't get into an accident with another driver, is that right?"

"Yeah, I – I don't know – I made a mistake. I shouldn't have been driving. I know."

"No, Abby. We know. You're not in trouble over that. We just want to know how your vehicle ended upside down almost fifty feet from the highway."

Fresh tears puddled up in the corners of her sockets. Both Aspen and Tucker leaned forward, knowing that any moment that shallow pool would overflow and the big break in the case would come soon after its contents spilled down her puffy cheeks. "I saw – I thought I saw something in the road," she choked, "it was a bright light, and then a shadow. It was probably a lizard or something, but the way the lights on my truck looked, it made the shadow seem– huge. I turned the wheel too far. I knew how to drive. My dad's been letting me drive his truck for almost a year. I–"

Tucker frowned, it seemed to him to be a step backwards, or at least in the wrong direction. Nevertheless, he continued on with the line of questioning as his partner robustly scribbled away in his pocket notebook. "Well, I guess we're particularly curious as to how *he* got there, now that we know who *he* is.

"Because we didn't at first. Not until we searched his truck and found his wallet. But the rest of the cab was empty, he didn't have a suitcase or packed bag, or even a toothbrush. We also had trouble locating his shipping papers. Plus, his trailer was empty. Which is strange because people in the industry have told me how difficult it is to maneuver a truck that size with an empty trailer. We've been playing phone tag with the people at his company. In fact, detective Aspen and myself are flying out to Sioux Falls tomorrow to talk with them."

Detective Tucker stopped, he felt a familiar hand reach out and poke him. He glanced over to find his partner looking at him in a frenzy, with his mouth agape.

Aspen mouthed the words, *what are you doing?*

Tucker shook his head.

This was not the normal route of interrogation. This was why the chief dragged the two of them into his office a few days before. He hollered a hole into their heads because they weren't investigating like they normally would. They were being sloppy. They weren't verifying facts with other agencies when they should have. They were forgetting to return phone calls and even called the same place twice. They were overlooking important leads. It seemed to the chief and the others that they were almost purposely screwing it up. It would be the only explanation for a pair of their caliber to be neglecting key factors like that.

A Need for Charlie

As Tucker was droning on, he felt like he were almost telling himself, trying to lay down and tidy up the facts of the case to keep it straight in his head. He recited their procedure like a rant, a confession – a therapy session.

But Abby had scarcely been paying attention, the sound of his voice had smoothed out and soothed her back to sleep. Also, the medication machine had administered more pain killer, causing her to drift in and out of consciousness.

Aspen threw down his pen in an almost disgusted manner. "I thought they told us that she would be ready for this." The detectives exchanged another awkward glance. It was not the way the interview was supposed to go. They had been tripped up by witnesses before, lost their footing momentarily, but not like this. Had Abby been more aware of her surroundings, they might have been more embarrassed.

"Okay fine, let's switch, but get it done. I don't want to have to come back here." Tucker muttered under his breath, trying desperately to get into game mode.

Aspen took charge, he gently shook her until her eyes opened at least half way again. "Abby, we need to ask you a few more questions, then we will leave you alone so you can get your rest."

"I'm sorry, I'm really tired," her voice had slowed to a whisper.

"I know, just try to concentrate for us, honey. This is really important. You're sure that you didn't crash into another vehicle?"

"Pretty sure."

"How sure? I mean – can you give me a percentage – a number maybe?"

"I don't know. It all happened so fast. I kept blacking out. I don't think I hit anything."

"Well, it's impossible for us to tell right now. We have forensics going over your truck with a fine toothed comb, but –" he stopped and took a sharp breath, realizing he was taking the same misstep as his partner, "that stuff takes a long time. Sometimes weeks. That's why we're here. We need to talk to you about it because you were the only person there."

"I guess I'm about sixty percent sure," she said after a while.

"Okay Abby. Now I'm going to ask you about Charlie. Do you know how much time passed between when you crashed and when he showed up?"

"I don't even know. I know the sun was going down when I crashed, but it was pitch black out when he was there."

"We know the sheriff's deputy found you the morning after you crashed, but can you try and guess how many hours it was until Charlie showed?"

"I don't know, I remember waking up, still in my seat. I was hanging upside down, in my seatbelt. But it hurt to move my legs. I remember waking up a second time and noticing that it was still night. I saw a few stars through the windshield, but it was cracked, so I couldn't see too many." Abby paused to sniff, the tears had found gravity and slid down her face.

Aspen passed her a Kleenex from a nearby box on the shelf. It sat next to a picture of her in a Halloween costume that looked like it was taken a few years ago. She was standing tall over a little boy on a bike who was wearing a cowboy hat and a toy gun saddle. "Is this is your little brother?" he held the frame out in front of her to lighten the mood.

"It's my – it's my nephew," she gasped in between sniffles.

"Oh, how old is he then?"

"He's six now. I gave him that bike for his fourth birthday."

"Oh, then you must be his favorite Auntie."

She sniffed, drying her tears. A subtle smile cracked her lips. "I'm his only one."

After he figured he got her back, Aspen continued, "Okay Abby. What happened when Charlie came upon your truck? Did he open the door right away? Did you hear him walking up?"

"No. I think my engine was still running. My foot was stuck, but I could move it a little. I think I pressed on the gas a few times. I know I heard the truck rev. I woke up a third time to this bright light, I opened my eyes and he was standing over me. I wasn't really scared. I knew he was big and all, but he seemed so nice, just by looking at him, I could tell he was a nice man. He was hurt too. He had blood on his cheek and when he moved around he fell once. I don't think I crashed into him, if that's what you're thinking."

Aspen shook his head, "No, his rig was parked very far away from your vehicle. In fact, it was parked so far away, I'm having a hard time understanding how he even saw your vehicle in the dark."

"Did you find him?" Abby asked, her actions and demeanor were becoming clearer. Her eyes still struggled a bit, but they were wide open.

Aspen and Tucker again exchanged mystified glances. Nothing was revealing itself the way they had hoped. Usually, in every interview there is at least one or two "ah-ha" moments. They don't customarily rely on eyewitness testimony, because human error runs rampant, but it frequently leads them to something else.

"Well – I mean – of course we found him. He was lying next to your truck face down in the dirt."

"Then he came back." It was a statement, but the way she phrased it, it sounded more like a question.

"What do you mean? Do you mean he left and then came back?"

"No, he left and didn't come back."

"Okay, we're getting ahead of ourselves here. What was said between the two of you. You did talk to him, didn't you Abby?" Aspen was sure that one would jar something loose in her collective memory.

"Yes."

"What was said?"

"He told me his name, and he told me he was there to watch over me. He told me that I would see my parents again, that I would play with my nephew in the yard. He told me that I was going to get my driver's license when I turn 16 next month. He told me that he would stay with me until someone else arrived. He told me a lot of things."

"Did you ask him to call an ambulance. Did he make any indication at all that he called for help?"

"He said he was going to help, but I don't think in that way. I don't know, it's so confusing. I didn't even think he was there some moments, but then other times I felt him touch me. I asked him to hold my hand, and he did. I fell asleep and he was still there, holding my hand, telling me all the things that I was going to do. He told me about college, and that one day I would get married and have kids. I think he told me that. And then he was gone. He didn't tell me he was leaving."

"Do you mean you woke up and he wasn't there?" Aspen asked, licking his lips. He noticed Tucker had stopped his feverish chicken scratch next to him, but he kept his eyes locked on Abby.

"No. When I woke up the second time he was there, the blood was gone from his face. He was holding my hand and smiling. I didn't know if I was dreaming – I –" Fresh tears began to roll down her cheeks again.

Aspen forcefully passed her another tissue. This time her sobs reached new levels. She murmured something in between blows into the tissue; Aspen thought it sounded like *I don't know*.

Eventually, the suspense was too much for him, "What Abby? What happened when you woke up the second time?"

"He just disappeared," she sobbed harder. This time, she reached an outstretched arm for the Kleenex box herself and jerked another pair of tissues out.

Tucker poked Aspen from behind like he had done to him earlier. He was so enthralled with her response that he nearly sprung up from his seat like a jack in the box. Tucker twirled his finger in the air at him, as if to say, *wrap it up, this is going nowhere.*

"What do you mean he disappeared Abby? Did he turn around and leave?"

"No," she shook her head, crying even harder. "He was there one minute and he was gone. H-huh-he j-juh-just dis-disappeared."

She was bordering on hysterics, and suddenly Aspen leaned back, becoming very uneasy. *How would this look right now if the nurse walked in?* he thought to himself.

He sighed, contemplating the jagged and fragmented bits of the interview. It had gone awry in more ways than one. There was nothing he or his partner could ask that would rectify it. It was simply the poorest interview two detectives of their tenure and track record could have conducted. Something bothered both of them about the case, and they were still no closer to cracking it. They couldn't put their finger on what was missing, but it slowly became apparent as they asked Abby their carefully constructed questions, they would not find the answer at Good Samaritan.

Aspen shook his head, "I guess I don't understand. I don't mean to badger you about this, but I've got to be crystal clear. You mean to tell me he disappeared into thin air?"

Abby couldn't answer, her emotions had taken over and were shaking her quite strenuously. She shook her head and rolled over to face the opposite way, "He saved me. He w-wuh-watched over me."

"That's enough," Tucker said from behind him. "Maybe we'll have better luck in South Dakota."

"I don't want to talk anymore," Abby muttered, sobbing a bit softer.

"That's fine, Abby. I'm sorry it was so difficult. We'll let you rest now." Aspen had felt the urge to pat her shoulder, but instead was being whisked out of the room by his partner before he got the chance. The last thing he saw before leaving her sight was a crucifixion card tied to a balloon, it read *GOD HAS BLESSED YOU.*

<u>8</u>

"Painful Awakenings"

Charlie awoke amidst a glinting sun and a pasty, blazing pain he never could have imagined. It closely resembled the sensation one gets when they stand too close to a bonfire – only it was all over, and more often than not, inside his body. He felt it was in the deteriorating stage, attacking the muscles in his legs. It could be felt on the side of his neck as it screamed when he turned his head for the first time after a long night on what turned out to be a dusty ground of a rail yard.

He got to his feet as slowly as a man who lived a hundred years might. The front of his face felt like someone poured a vat of nitric acid on it. Almost like his skin was sagging and liquefying. Thankfully, a headache wasn't in the cards. Charlie rarely got them, even after a night of drinking. He was always more prone to body aches for a hangover, and he had those anyhow.

It was hot– maybe ninety degrees already. The only clouds in the kingdom of the blue sky were the harmless, puffy ones. Charlie squinted at the rusty railroad ties, trying to work out his position. His vision was slow at working its way back to him. Instantly, he had already decided he would not walk back past the *Leatherneck*, even if he *could* find it.

Then it suddenly came to him, he was looking at the Burlington Northern tracks that border I-80. He turned around and off in the flat distance was the afternoon commute. It was probably two miles away. The station where the monster ten was parked couldn't have been more than five.

Charlie tried to sigh, but it came out as more of a hacking cough. He hawked one up and spat, grimacing at more of those aches and pains it caused. He felt something fall from the roof of his mouth and it dropped sharply on his tongue. He opened his jaws grudgingly and removed one of his teeth from the incubator of his taste buds. He stared at it for a moment, the intense light of the day didn't paint a flattering portrait of it. It was scummy and yellow, stained from years of puffing on Reds.

After a swarm of mosquitoes buzzed swiftly past him, he did his best Nolan Ryan impression with his limited movement and hurled it at the railroad track. It hit the rusty rail dead-on. (TINK!)

He took it one step at a time, until his body got used to the movement. Whether it liked it or not, he was going to have to hump back out to the scales. There was no soft hearted, young bullhauler to rescue him this time.

His only hope was a string of passing boxcars, but even if he was that lucky, he wasn't too sure his body would be limber enough to hop on.

He was still dog-tired and desperately needed a shower. In fact, his stank was so pungent that it could've been detected within a hundred feet. He touched his face, but instantly pulled away as if it were scalding hot. There was a burning sensation all right, it was felt on the very tip of his cheek. His fingers were splattered with an almost yellowish gooey substance on them. It reminded Charlie of the puss that flows from a whitehead or ingrown hair. But what he felt underneath his fingertips for the briefest of moments was hard– like a boil or a cyst. It stung; but it couldn't have helped that he was sleeping face down in the dust after a night of heavy drinking.

Once everything started to gel again, Charlie began to speed walk since the sweat was pouring so profusely anyhow. To try and take his mind of the pain he thought about all the events that occurred within the last twenty-four hours. As hurt as he was, he was still able to stir up an ounce of fury in his aching bones. His windpipe still felt like it was leaning, but thinking how this was all the work of that *goddamn injun*, he felt he could still breathe fire through it. He thought about all these things and others, wondering in a voice that was the total antithesis of Charlie, if this would be his last trip.

'*Last stop! End of the line!*' it screamed.

Just then he pictured a word in mid air – it could have been a mirage even – it was large and looming like it had been written on his papers.

TEMPE.

This ol' rig has ran over its last cat! It has screamed on by its mile-marker! It has grinded its last gear! Is that a 10-4, good buddy?

<u>9</u>

"On the Road Again"

Four grueling hours later, Charlie was finally sweating through the vinyl seat of the monster ten. He never thought he would have been so happy to see its scowling, faded face. Charlie felt a cold, refreshing wave wash over him as he felt the wind of freedom scream through his window when crossing the border into Nebraska– another sight that was surprisingly for sore eyes.

He had rolled both windows down as he waited to pull out of the last DOT garage he ever wanted to lay eyes on. The sweet smell of endless prairie, corn and cow manure was favored over the stank that wafted from his pores. Even when he showed up for his rig, the DOT bear took a double take at Charlie and practically shoved him into his truck, pinching his nose all the way.

Thank Christ that injun bitch wasn't there.

The thought of her didn't occur to Charlie until a few miles down I-80. But even when she showed up in his mind, she left just as suddenly. She disappeared in a puff of campfire smoke, amistd a lolling of wordless chants.

Charlie laughed out loud– it hurt, but it felt good in a way too. He watched the sun creep below the horizon as he opened the pocket of his denim jacket and pulled out a crumpled pack of Reds. Then he remembered the pack he left behind after telling off the injun. It laid sprawled out in the corner of the dashboard, the deep red color fading after hours in the baking Iowa sun. The pack he had with him at the *Leatherneck* only contained one salvageable stick, so Charlie lit it up and tossed the wounded soldiers out the window. He felt DAMN good. Nothing was going to stop him now.

By the time he reached Lincoln, he couldn't stand his own smell any longer. He figured it a good time to stop and stretch his legs anyhow. So he picked a truck stop just off the Homestead Expressway on the south end of town. Slowly, he searched his bag to make sure the DOT pigs didn't steal

any of his stuff, not that it was worth a damn to anybody but him. But he

figured they may have anyway, in defense of the wicked heathen who fined

him nearly a week's pay.

It was all there. After a minute or two of inventory, he grabbed a new

pair of shorts, jeans and a t-shirt and moseyed into the shower facilities.

There was only one other truck in the lot and he wasn't inside, Charlie had

the place to himself. It was a good thing too, he nearly jumped right out of

his skin when he saw what stared back at him in the mirror. The thing on his

face had nearly doubled in size. It looked like it was growing underneath,

creating a dark, brooding dome right on the tip of his cheek. Not to mention

the serious purple bruise along side his face and the dried up trickle of blood

on his forehead that resembled an ancient rusty, desert riverbed. He felt like

he had to heave, only there wasn't anything in his stomach to heave. He

bent to his knees, wondering exactly what moment in time he had stopped

looking after his health.

Had he ever?

When *was* the precise moment that he gave up on everything?

After a moment or two, he felt better and stood up. He showered

quickly, clearing the dust caked on his face and brightening the few bruises he had on his body. Glory wounds from the battle the night before. He changed and felt millions better. Even the thing on his face seemed to breathe a little easier. It was merely red now, much less jarring than the colors he saw before.

When he was done washing up and buying an extra pack of Reds from a machine, he got back out to his rig and decided he wouldn't drive another mile. He ran his fingers through his greasy hair and looked up at the dark sky. Little lights were winking at him from above, a soft breeze whirled along through the vast open landscape. Charlie didn't want to sit the rest of the night in the ugly worn down monster, so he decided to do something he hadn't done in at least five years. He climbed his tractor, nearly fell off, but eventually he was able to lie on the top of his trailer, letting the breeze rush across his sore body.

Of course, twenty years ago he would do it in the middle of the day. When summer hit he would schedule his breaks around high noon, that way he could rid himself of the shadows on his arms from sitting in the rig all day. He'd flip over every ten minutes to keep the tan even, smoking a Red when he was on his back. Charlie was quite vein in his day, back when the lot lizards were a lot slimmer for the pickings. Back then, he wanted to look good for them. They gave him the only thing he ever *needed* from a woman.

He got it plenty too – he had nothing else to spend his money on, and he would ration that it was much cheaper than a family would cost.

He would lie on his trailer every damn day from April to October– out there in his playground. He remembered how hot the tops of the shiny new cabooses would get on his back if he shifted even an inch or two outside his shadow. He remembered how his skin smelled after hours in the sun, almost damp and dewy. On several occasions he wound up being so relaxed up there, he would fall asleep to the sounds of diesel engines roaring past him on the highway. He remembered one occasion in August of some far off year, he was in the middle of the Mohave, he passed out and nearly slept three hours on his back. When he awoke, he became terribly sick. He heaved his guts out onto the red earth, almost got stung by a scorpion and had just enough gas to drive himself to the nearest hospital, which at that time was still fifty miles away.

He remembered the next time he was back in Sioux Falls, after his hospital stint he got together with the fellas for some cards. During the game he ran around with his shirt off, showcasing his new brown, crispy complexion. "Don't I look mah-lah-to? Look at me, I look like I just crawled a hundred miles under trip wire to cross the border into

Brownsville! I look like the fucking broad who's in denial over her mehn-no-pause! I look like a light vision of buckwheat!"

"You certainly brag like a nigger," Rhiney yelled at him when he was itching to call his full house.

A bray of cattle calls off in the distance interrupted Charlie's stream of thoughts long buried. The sun had been down a while, but something still burned on the back of his neck. It was the sweltering scorch of regret. He regretted laying up there all those times.

He lit a Red and thought about it some more. *Maybe I outta spaced em' out more*, he thought. *I coulda layed up there on some nights too, just like now. Look at this shit I was missing.*

No matter how many Reds he choked down, Charlie never stopped thinking about it. It ate at him long after he retreated into the not-so-cozy-confines of the monster ten. He couldn't remember for sure, but he may have even dreamed of being burned alive. Sprawled out over the bright, shimmery desert that was the Mohave– steaming– waiting for the buzzards to brave the one hundred and twenty degree heat and pick at his charred remains.

<u>10</u>

"Sleeping in the Bed you Made"

He awoke in cold sweats, his face stinging worse than ever before. It wasn't until he began moving along I-80 again did he feel better.

Maybe I can still finish this trip off strong, he thought to himself around Grand Island.

And after a short while, even Charlie believed he had found his footing on the trip. As the miles on the odometer rolled on and Lexington gave way to North Platte, Charlie was downright chipper. He rarely had to down or upshift, another beauty of driving through Nebraska at a conservative seventy-five. He was sore, but the wind whipping through the window numbed the pain. And the most important thing, he was finally getting some miles under his belt.

TEMPE.

The words puffed out onto the highway in front of him again, like red smoke breathing out of the asphalt, just as they had looked on his papers. Old Hal knew he didn't like trips to the desert in the August heat. His skin couldn't take it anymore.

Darla-the-dyke changed it, I could practically see the fuckin' white-out drying before my eyes.

Somewhere around Ogallala he decided it was time to take another break. His bladder was pleading with him to choke the snake, and even though it wasn't running on fumes, the monster ten was still getting low on gas. Charlie figured he might as well get it in Nebraska. *The farther west you go the worse the prices get these days.*

The sun was again bedding itself down for the evening. The day had flown by as fast as the yardsticks when Charlie pushed the ten past seventy-five, trying to find out what she could muster. He soon realized he hadn't filled in the lines on his comic book, he puffed on a Red and went to work on it. Already he had driven over the maximum eight hour limit, and didn't take a break in between either. He worked at his log, following all the safe rules mandated by the DOT pricks. But Charlie never bothered to abide by them fully. He was from the old school of driving and everyone who was anyone in that particular class knew that nothing was going to change his ways. He laughed loudly to himself when that thought crept up, it made him feel old, but somehow– it was okay.

A brief half hour nap followed, nothing serious, just something to tide him over. He would always try and drive the mountains at night – if he could. It wasn't that he didn't appreciate their majestic beauty, it was merely one of those unwritten rules he wrote and lived by. He always handled the grades with the expert skill he had accumulated over the years from really the only profession that mattered to him.

He decided right then and there he wanted to get to Tempe as quickly as possible.

No– he *needed* to get there.

Once he crossed the state border on I-76 and drove right into the clutches of Mountain Time, Charlie had a certain bent appeal that he may just drive all the way through the night.

DOT bears and chicken coops and evil fire-worshipping injuns and hemorrhoids with Polaroids be damned, he smirked and then spat out his window.

He was feeling that old familiar giddiness he often enjoyed in his earlier days of driving. The way the engine screamed on command from his foot, the way the turbocharger would spool up and force air into the engine, hissing all the way when Charlie would punch it. The way the white noise sounded off when Sesame Street became a ghost-town. The way the ass end of the trailer would swing into the hammer lane on a sharp curve. And to a lesser extent, although he wasn't going to see them at night, the way kids on family trips would jerk their arms endlessly in the air, petitioning him to honk the horn.

Several other moments blew through his mind, all happy, all taking place in his borderless playground.

There was the time he joined forces with a couple of guys from Texas and forced a smart-mouthed rookie that talked *too* smart on channel 19 off the road and onto one of those gravel infested escape ramps, driving down into Parley's Canyon outside Salt Lake City. The kid was trying to show up Charlie and the other veterans, flying down the steep grade, whizzing past them in a fury.

The trio caught up to him halfway down, one of the fellas from Texas did the pushing, where Charlie flanked the rear to keep him from stopping. It worked like a charm, the kid slammed into the gravel ramp spewing out tiny bits of pebbles and dust behind him. It was a glorious explosion in that when the dust settled, the food chain was clear again.

Charlie was young in those days, but not as young as the rook. When he expressed the slightest bit of regret to the other rig, the man responded in his heavy-handed, deep-seeded drawl: *Ya sleep in da bed you make, son.*

Right on, Charlie, not wanting to let the Texans down responded after a sigh.

He never heard from either of them again, but the man's words always stuck with him for some reason. At the time, it struck Charlie as an odd saying. He thought about it often and even used it himself a time or two over his career. But what did he really mean by it? You get what you give? You reap what you sew? Was it a comment on environment and how it manipulates you?

No...*Ya sleep in da bed you made, son.*

But what if someone else made the bed for you? Would Charlie still have to sleep in it, then?

Would he *need* to sleep in it?

For some reason, he tried to think back as far as his mind could travel and came to the conclusion that he never was really happy until he discovered his playground. He could never conjure up a lucidly happy memory unless it involved him manning the wheel of a big rig.

Charlie drew in a deep, raspy breath of the musky, Eastern Colorado air. That sweet smelling oxygen that was about to get a whole lot thinner a hundred miles down the road. But still he could not think of it. It's as if time and the effects of several hundred seven-seven's over the years had blocked it all out.

Not all the times had been good for Charlie, both recent and long ago. In fact, some hadn't been very good at all.

He scratched at his face until it bled, not just a trickle, but enough for a small sponge to absorb. Then he thought of that phrase again, and also something that resembled environment.

Ya sleep in da bed you made, son.

<u>11</u>

"The Shack under the Silver Moon"

She slammed through a deep, ill-timed pothole in the road; not enough to pull over to check the struts, but enough for her bottle of scotch to spill, causing her to curse everyone under the sun. Mariann Coldbrick pulled the rusty '55 Bel-air into the gravel driveway of the shack she called home– the one she shared with her husband and young son. She took him on trips into town often, it was the only entertainment they could afford. But it was more often than not an ample opportunity for her to grab some hooch at a cheap price. They lived off Route 38 on the west end of town, a spit's length from the city limits.

On this particular night Mariann was gracious enough to pick up two and half pounds of shredded beef for the week from the butcher. It certainly wasn't enough for all three of them, but they had just a little under no money.

Mariann was quite a looker in her day, but by the time Charlie reached the age of seven her skin begun to sag, her eyes puffed, and her shiners would be all the more discolored because of it. Charlie always looked at her from a chilled, objective view. Not only as an adult, but especially as a child. Young Charlie always studied her, constantly pilfering through the elements that made up her character. She was his mother, and half of his sole model of the human race after all. He needed her during that time, and every once in a while, on that particular day – she was there for him.

"Hand me that," she motioned frantically with her aging hand at the brown paper bag of shredded beef. Charlie, wide eyed and breathing lightly handed her the stained, crumpled bag that dripped tiny spots of blood onto the faded and degraded vinyl seat of the Bel-Air.

"Jesus," she wiped at it, clicking off the radio when it went to a broadcast commercial.

"Mama?" young Charlie asked in a tiny voice that he hadn't grown into yet.

"What?" she was annoyed and agitated already, and it wasn't even ten PM yet.

"Why ain't we going inside?"

"We're waitin'," she suspiciously eyed another vehicle parked ten feet down the driveway. A newer, lily white version of a Galaxy. It held half a dozen grocery bags in its back seat, it shimmered in the night– the moon was full.

"What we waitin' for?" Charlie asked once he built up the courage to do so.

She didn't answer him. Instead, she took another swig from her brown bottle and lit up a *Lucky Strike*. Silence was between them for a while. Charlie grabbed himself near his midsection, wincing at some undetermined pain. But Mariann sat with smoke billowing off her breath and watched indistinct shadows amble around in jerky movements inside their shack.

"Mama?"

"WHAT IS IT?" she seethed, jerking her head around and burning pinholes with her eyes through his body.

"I have to go to the bathroom," he held his midsection firmer to illustrate.

"Then get the fuck out and go behind the shed. Squeeze your little pecker 'til it's dry. Whado I care? But don't go anywhere near the house, ya hear?"

He sat and watched her for another moment, on the verge of sniffles and dewy eyes. *How can she be so mean?* Charlie thought at the time. *How can she when we just had the best-est time together? It's me, I made her mad – somehow. She went somewhere with me and bought me beef from the butcher and now I made her mad.*

"Do you want me to stay here?" he asked, trying to make up for his seemingly wrong doing.

"No one needs anything from you. No one will EVER need anything from you! Your-" her rabid voice vibrated, "Your just like your father."

"I'm sorry, mama," his voice tried to remain strong for her, but it was on the verge of slipping at any moment. Charlie didn't want to cry, he wanted to do anything but that. It just would have made her madder.

"Don't be fuckin' sorry, you little schlitz – just GO!" she paused to drag off her Lucky, "Don't slam the door neither or I'll beat your butt in!"

And Charlie went. He zig zagged around the car that was foreign to them, he may have showed it more interest if he hadn't had to pee. Quickly, he ran around the side of the shed like he was told. He did it facing the glassy, open night air. There was a bit of a brisk wind for it being May, but even by that age Charlie knew that the sun would beat down tomorrow and it would be hot. As hot a summer day as the Dakota wind could possibly provide.

Normally, he didn't enjoy being outside after dark. Because around their shack, dark was darkest. They weren't near the city, they had tall maples surrounding the acre of property they had left. And every so often Mariann or her husband, Butch, forgot to pay the electricity bill. However, at that moment in time, as he let three glasses of kool-aid slowly leak out of him, Charlie developed his first appreciation ever for the natural world. Of what it might have to offer. He had a bit of a curious personality, he wanted to explore what was out there – his future playground.

He never played outside with other kids unless he was at school because they didn't live near any. But on that night, Charlie didn't mind it a bit. He stood gazing at the full moon, large and looming on the horizon. Some kid named Scottie in his class once claimed a man's face was visible on it. He also claimed it was made out of cheese and only astronauts could eat it. Charlie stood there in the gentle breeze, whizzing, trying to decide for himself if there was a face.

But a thump from around front jolted his train of thought. It nearly stopped his piss cold in its tracks – no easy feat. He heard bantering and then a screeching noise, it sounded like his mother's voice. Then a loud crash followed afterward, the sound of metal banging against a cheap, vinyl linoleum floor.

When Charlie came around the short side of the shed, he came face to face with that of a younger, healthier woman. He thought he recognized her in the moonlight as their neighbor from a couple miles down the road, Mrs. Juniper. She stopped when she met young Charlie's eyes, he wasn't sure if he scared her or if she was going to be mean to him too. Her eyes were completely bloodshot and soaked, a bit of mascara ran from their corners.

"Hi," Charlie's high soothing voice called out to her from the darkness.

She didn't return the pleasantry. Instead, she stood there and stared at him for another moment. As his eyes adjusted to the darker front yard, he noticed her dress was torn and her hair was messed up. It looked to Charlie as if she had been sleeping on it, the way his mother's curls looked when he got home from school.

A stifled sob escaped her lips, it was so piercing and sudden that Charlie nearly fell over from surprise. Another one slipped out and soon she couldn't contain any of it. Tears streaked down her cheeks and her wailing

voice could be heard amidst the crickets and the slight wind flapping sound

of bats overhead. She looked quite sad to Charlie, but he also thought she

looked like she didn't know what she was doing. She looked like she was

half crazy or trying to decide between two important decisions.

Just as suddenly as she stopped, she jumped into the lily white Galaxy

and jetted off down the gravel drive, casting one last look back into

Charlie's confused and befuddled eyes. He watched as the tail lights

disappeared around the maples that boarded the Coldbrick's property.

Was mommy mean to her? Is that why she's sad? Charlie wondered

silently to himself.

The loudest crash yet escaped out from behind the cheap walls of the

shack. Several heavy objects sounded like they had crashed triumphantly to

the ground. Charlie knew what was coming, but he decided to go in

anyway. He would always eventually have to, if he wanted to sleep or eat or

up until recently, watch TV (his mother sold the brand new television his

father bought a couple days prior) he would have to go in. He could hear his

mother's voice first, it was ranting in nonsensical syllables. A fainter,

deeper voice answered back between sharp gasps of breath.

Charlie pulled open the screen door and braced himself.

"..others? Huh?! HOW MANY OTHER WHORES ARE THERE? YOU ARE USELESS! AHB-SO-LUHT-LEY USELESS!" Mariann screamed at her husband who was getting up off the kitchen floor, a large rusty frying pan lay next to his arm.

"I SURE AS SHIT AM NOT!!! WOULD WE HAVE ALL THIS IF I WAS USELESS?!! HUH?! WOULD YOU BE UP TO YOUR ASS IN BOTTLES OF SCOTCH EVERY NIGHT IF I DIDN'T DO A GODDAMN THING ALL DAY!"

"I GUESS NOT ALL OF YOU IS USELESS!" she kicked at him, but he easily dodged it, sending her reeling backwards until she almost fell over. "AT LEAST I KNOW SOMEBODY'S GETTING SOME USE OUTTA YOU! YOU FUCKING BASTARD!!!! HOW MANY ARE THERE? HOW MANY OTHERS?" she was screaming at the top of her lungs now, her voice sounded like it was on the brink of total meltdown. It seemed like the walls would have caved in if she uttered one more hoarse word.

"AT LEAST THEY'RE ALIVE! AT LEAST I CAN TELL THAT BLOOD STILL PUMPS THROUGH THEIR VEINS, UNLIKE SOME PEOPLE!! WITH THEM, AT LEAST IT'S NOT LIKE FUCKIN' A CORPSE!" Butch shouted back at her, although only matching half of her volume and intensity.

"OH! OH! OH! THEN WHAT THE FUCK IS IT, HUH? WHAT FLOWS THROUGH MY VEINS, THEN!"

He looked her up and down, a look of complete disdain and disgust. It was as if he were looking at the contents of a recently deposited septic tank. "By the smell of it," his voice calmed, "Scotch."

"OH FUCK YOOU! YOU HEAR ME YOU LIMP DICK! YOU THINK YOU'RE SO FUCKIN' GOOD! YOU'RE THE ONLY MAN IN THE WHOLE WORLD BESIDES THE GODDAMN AMISH WHO DON'T DRINK! HELL, EVEN A PRIEST WILL SLOSH 'EM DOWN WITH THE REST OF 'EM! PFFFT! MR. PERFECT!!"

At that precise moment, she noticed Charlie out the corner of her eye, sneaking behind them, attempting to creep quietly to his room. "Where the FUCK do you think you're going?"

He froze instantly, he always did when she directed that tone at him. He didn't have the power to answer her, so he cautiously studied her frosty exterior. Charlie sometimes imagined he had an invisibility belt like in the comics he read. That way, when she looked at him like that (mean), he could look right back and disappear before her very eyes. If he were gone, then it was only plausible to young Charlie that the look on her face (mean) would disappear as well.

She made a move toward him, "I THOUGHT I TOLD YOU TO STAY OUTSIDE!!" Looking at him like a bull, a piece of her straggly hair bounced in her face, she was so furious by that point that she practically ripped it out of her head to move it.

The only thing that stopped her from accosting the boy and throwing him as far across the room as her drunken strength would allow was Butch. He grabbed her by the arm and spun her back to where she was, almost as if it were an intricate move in a very complex tango.

He rarely ever laid a hand on her. Although, he may have taken it upon himself to give her a whoopin' once every so often. But long ago, he decided there was no point. He would take her abuse as the lark that it was. He knew neither of them could afford a divorce, not that she would take the initiative anyhow, as long as he kept her liver deep in scotch. What he would do was cheat on her every chance he got– and for that– Charlie eventually decided to hate him more so than his mother. But on the other side, Butch loved his son, he rarely was ever able to provide much for him, but he loved him all the same. That is why the only time he ever intervened with his wife's insanity was when she would try and take it out on Charlie.

"DON'T YOU LOOK AT HIM! YOU LOOK AT ME!" It was then his turn to unleash fury.

But Mariann would have none of it, "YOU FUCKIN' PIG!!! YOU LIMP-DICKED LITTLE FAGGOT!" she began to wail on him, tightening both of her clenched fists into balls of fire.

Butch would allow her to go on for a while sometimes, if it was enough for her to pass out he would take it. The peace and quiet was always worth what never amounted to more than a few bruises. "You leave him outta this!" he yelled at her as she went to town.

She stopped and looked up, "He's gonna turn out just like you! A pathetic, whiny excuse for a husband! A limp dick!"

"Oh no he's not," Butch was actually able to smile a bit at this, "Father's always want a better life for their sons – well watch this!" He shoved her back and walked gently over to Charlie.

"Charlie," he placed his hand on his son's shoulder so he would look away from his mother.

"What daddy?"

"DON'T EVER GET MARRIED!" he shouted, loud enough for her to hear. Then his voice turned to a whisper, "Look what can happen," he patted him on the shoulder and giggled. "You hear me, boy? Whatever you do, don't get married. Look what can happen to you."

"YEAH! GO AHEAD!" Mariann chimed in, only half aware she was speaking at all. "GO AHEAD AND LISTEN TO YOUR FAH-THER. Be just like him, be half a man with a limp dick who can't even provide for his family! A man no one in the world needs anything from." She charged at her husband again.

He was ready for her and gave her a violent shove backwards, she tripped over her own heels and crashed to the floor. Butch then turned toward his son and scooted him in the direction of his bedroom, "Go to bed," he commanded.

When he turned around he was met with that malevolent scream that sent the windows rattling, the stars stumbling and the world spinning. She tried to give him a chop to the adam's apple, but missed and hit the side of his face instead. He placed a hairy palm over her withered mouth and flung her back again, allowing her another visit to the floor.

"YOU BASTARD!!!" That blood curdling voice rang out at top volume. Her eyes were in a frenzy as her hands searched frenetically on the floor for something…anything. Finally her hands came upon her bottle of scotch with nary a sip left, she wound up, and threw a fastball at her husband.

Because of her slowness from the booze, he was able to duck and dodge it easily. It flew through the air in what seemed like slow motion, it twirled end over end in a dizzying display of physics. It flew majestically like a bird floating in a thick Dakota wind. The emptiness of it caught the right kind of air and it whistled sharply as it flew. It shrieked and soared until it stopped– until it shattered on the skull of young Charlie Coldbrick.

<u>12</u>

"A Need for Charlie"

Somewhere around Sterling, Charlie let out a deep gasp of air. Once the memory of that long forgotten night crept up on him, he couldn't escape its powerful grip. It seemed to put him in a trancelike state. The past had been doing an awful lot of that for Charlie lately.

He thought once again about environment, also about the sun in the Mohave. *How come this comes back to me now?* he thought to himself.

I need this. I need this like I need to get pulled over by BP carryin' a wagon full of Mexicans.

"Jesus," he muttered softly to himself. Slyly, as if someone were watching, he pulled a Red from the front pocket of his jacket.

Charlie had seldomly given his parents a second thought for quite some time. Whenever he did, it was in quick retrospect, although it left a sour aftertaste that often lasted days. He joined the marines when he was seventeen and never looked back. Once he was discharged, he soon discovered his playground and the rest was history. That had been okay with Charlie up until now. There was just one thing lacking, a missing link somewhere on the map.

No one will ever *need anything from you.*

He choked on his Red and decided he didn't want it anymore. Letting the wind in again, he tossed it, littering his own personal Mecca. But suddenly Charlie felt very agitated. Meaning to reach for the knob to turn up Sesame Street, his hand went its own way and scratched at his face. It no longer stung, it felt prickly all over and beyond. It felt like little charges of electricity were going off around and within it. New bits of skin and blood replaced the old under his fingernails, he needed to trim them. His left middle pierced it so hard that he cried out in pain and nearly broke a cardinal ruling of trucking.

Don't never take both hands off the wheel of this or any rig, use your head! A crabby trucking instructor Charlie once had screamed at him through a toothpick during his two week training course.

You sleep in da bed you made, son.

That's what it was and Charlie knew it too. He wasn't quite ready to admit it to himself. Not just yet. He never *would* need to either, if it hadn't been for his vacation.

That's what it was for Charlie. He *needed* some kind of dependence, if only for a little while. It was a sensation most fulfill before they reach the age of ten, but Charlie had never even had a whiff of it, let alone a taste. He never wanted a family, everyone who ever knew him would tell you it was a wise decision on his part. Grand illusions that he was the oil for the engine of American industry was just something truckers would use to justify their job. Everyone does it.

Did Charlie actually believe it?

Probably not. He didn't believe in much– and no matter how many times he was hit in the head, he never thought that the world wouldn't live without him. That was just the problem. What Charlie needed was to be needed, and his playground didn't really cut it.

Many times the harsh, realistic notion had entered his mind on any one or all of America's highways and byways.

If it wasn't me, they'd just tattoo some other asshole with a hazmat and send em' on his way.

13

"Worlds of White Hot Pain"

Charlie had become so restless that he decided right then and there he wouldn't be visiting Denver that night. The ten was eerily quiet the last few hours between Sterling and Fort Morgan. It became an annoying drone that drilled between his ears until he finally settled on a stop with a diner. His stomach growled for flapjacks. It wasn't until he pulled out the yellow diamond and the old familiar sound of air hissing sounded off that he thought about DOT bears getting a hold of him. They would give it to him

nice and proper

ten times harder than the injun. Probably pull his pull his hazmat right out from under his legs, spoiling an altogether wretched trip that was cursed from the beginning anyhow. He expressed his best storytelling capabilities the only way he knew how, by drawing lines and filling in the gibberish in his comic book.

Ready for another Red, he reached into his pocket ready to light up and go in. He figured he wouldn't press his luck and would at least wait till the next afternoon to even think about going again. Maybe he would eat a couple meals at the diner, he could shower and possibly shave. He planned all of those things in the moment he reached for a Red, but he did none of them. Instead, he fell calmly and serenely asleep. Anxious to cast himself out of the world of white hot pain and memories of eternal life and into the land of ancient slumber.

That night Charlie had the same dream as before. He was lying in the sun, the rusty red Mohave was so blinding that he caught only a flash of it before it forever darkened his vision. But there was something different about it, it came right at the end. A couple hundred yards away from where he parked his rig in the loneliest pickle park under the sun. The desert was vast and sprawling, but in an area not too far from where Charlie laid beet red atop of his metal throne, a cloud of dust emerged from nothing. It may have been the tail of a snake spanking the earth. There may have been a tiny air pocket of wind that rustled up a region of dust before bedding it back down again. Whatever the cause was, Charlie couldn't tell from the dream.

But moments before the big, bright, yellow sun scorched Charlie's retinas,

he saw it in the cloud of dust. The wind manipulated the fine sand just

enough to spell a word out in mid air. TEMPE.

The moment the dream went black, a ringing blew out from

somewhere above. It may have been the sound the sun makes when it

finally burns out. It may have been the strong desert wind caving in the side

of Charlie's trailer. The ringing turned to smashing, which gave way to

thumping. The sound of a heavy fist beating hard against the driver's

window of his rig.

<u>14</u>

"Curious Confidants"

His eyes burst open as if ignited by some kind of black powder, the

sun *was* there– right along with the world. It was mid morning already, and

the barren parking lot Charlie left behind one night previous had suddenly

become a clusterfuck. There wasn't a cloud in the sky, but the tips of white

shroudy mountains were visible just to the west. Also, the parking lot had

the brown filtered haze of diesel smoke billowing every which way by the gaggle of tractors screaming in and out of the lot. It was filled to the brim with the cantankerous, shrewd yells of greasy truckers and mountain folk, taking a break from the playground or going about their daily business.

But none of that interested Charlie, the only thing that did was the set of stubby knuckles banging on his window. He turned his head and locked eyes with a frighteningly familiar face.

It was Rhiney, his old buddy he hadn't seen in the better part of three years. They looked to Charlie like they had been tough years at that. The last time they spoke was on uncomfortable terms. They had made a bet on the Superbowl, a gentleman's agreement, but never shook on it. Charlie lost and took the low road, citing the bet was never finalized due to the lack of a handshake.

Stupid really, Charlie thought to himself as he reached for the handle to open the squeaky door of the ten. Soon after that, Rhiney had gotten a new gig with *Superfreight*. With that came all kinds of great benefits that would allow him to retire within the next five years.

Not Charlie though, because of all the noise he had made over his infamous career, he'd have been lucky to retire before he reached triple digits. That gold watch never seemed so far away.

The moment he moved, his back screamed at him in pain. He had slept sitting in the captain's chair all night, and his marrow had become rusty because of it.

He winced as he climbed out, as soon as the fresh wind hit his face he was reminded of the blinding torture in the Mohave again. His face recoiled in terror, feeling like it could shrivel up like a raisin in the sun. It even hurt to smile, not that Charlie did very much. But seeing the albeit languished face of his friend had momentarily brought back happier memories for him.

"Color me rusty," Rhiney cleared a frog from his throat. "Jesuit, I thought I'd 'ave to bust your goddamn window to get'u awake!"

"It's been a long time," Charlie still studied him with a cautious demeanor, he wasn't sure of the terms they'd be on. "Everything right on? You ain't still mad about the Superbowl?" Charlie always had a way of cutting through the B.S. that made Rhiney bust a gut or a toothpick on more than one occasion.

"Cripes!" Rhiney rattled a sour breath between his teeth, which suggested to Charlie that he had recently awakened as well. "FUCK the Superbowl!"

"You'on a run then, ain't ya?"

"Yes sir, on my way down to Tallahassee."

A Need for Charlie

Charlie cringed for a moment. It was the bitterness he felt toward Darla the dyke still churning within him, remembering his five was down there in the sunshine state. He briefly turned back to look at the ten, its pouty face still grimaced like Charlie's.

Can't wait to be rid of the fuckin' thing.

When it became abundantly clear to Rhiney that Charlie had remained a man of few words, just like the old days, he asked, "Then where you headed, hotsnot?"

TEMPE. The words billowed up in the dust of Charlie's dream, and then gave way to the blackest blanket of dark that ever veiled his eyes.

He ignored the question, instead he lit the first Red of the morning. "You want to get some breakfast? I don't remember the last time I so much as thought of food. Wha'daya say, Rhine?"

<u>15</u>

"Breakfast with Rhiney"

Charlie sneered at the waitress, a young, wiry girl in her twenties. He figured she was new on account of her stumbling and fumbling her words. "I said three flat tires and a couple of headlights," his sneer developed into a smirk.

The girl made a perfect o with her mouth, she looked as if she were about to become ill. Finally, Rhiney intervened and explained it meant three pancakes and two eggs, sunny-side up. But Charlie sure got a kick from making her feel ill like that, he saw it in her face. He also believed he could tell what kind of woman she would become.

Only one goddamned kind.

"I'm fine with the coffee," Rhiney smiled at her, trying to calm her nerves.

But she only looked at Charlie, she was fixated on his face.

The smirk quietly faded from it when he realized what it was. Rhiney had given him a similar, yet subtler look when he watched Charlie climb gracelessly out of his ten. The rest of his face flushed a bit, which always pissed him off when anyone, especially a woman, was able to humiliate him like that. After another moment he was able to regain enough composure to croak out, "Bye," when she wouldn't leave.

She rocketed back to the kitchen so fast that she nearly knocked over an elderly lady dressed in a windbreaker and pushing a walker.

"She's lucky she didn't trip over her own damn legs," Rhiney guffawed, slowly twisting the toothpick between his lips. Charlie noticed he had on the same dusty green cap he had worn for years both on and off the road. Rhiney had gone bald when he was twenty years old, he was so ashamed that he always wore a hat. Charlie figured, *by now his head must be starting to grow around that ugly, old thing.*

"Ahh," Charlie grunted, "fuck 'er." Nervously, he itched at his face and looked down at the marble table outfitted with a Plexiglas top, stained with ketchup and littered with crumpled napkins.

"So I see you ain't changed *much*," Rhiney picked at his teeth more aggressively.

"Naw," Charlie snorted, lighting another Red.

"Well, whatcha been doing, Coldbrick?" Rhiney's voice twinged.

"Just working, man. Cause that's what I am. A workin' mahn."

"How's ol' Hal treatin' ya?"

Charlie chuckled, sloppily flicking his ash in the tray, "Damn-dest thing, Rhine. Actually the whole fuckin' thing has been damned from the start," he stopped and stared like the waitress had. He figured Rhiney probably thought he had become a schiz-o. "That's what started this whole thing."

"I don't read ya." Rhiney puzzled at him, but he didn't look at him as if he were nuts like Charlie thought he might. Instead, he watched him like a boy burning an ant with a magnifying glass in the sun, a sort of morbid curiosity as he went on picking his teeth.

"That's what started the whole goddamn trip, the fact that I walked through that door and Hal wasn't there."

"Where'd he go to?" Rhiney looked genuinely interested.

"He got canned or somethin'," Charlie shrugged, "I don't know, he just ain't there. But this fuckin' bulldog dyke is there, sittin' behind Hal's desk, in Hal's chair, and starts barkin' orders at me as if I was the dog."

"What? What'd she say?"

"Nothin' worth repeating, just that she's in and Hal's out."

"Be careful, women like that like to make examples outta guys like you. We're a dying breed, Charlie. You and me. Their phasing us out. Like what they doin' to me. They ain't *offering* me early retirement. They makin' me retire. I'm gonna miss this."

"When are you done?"

"End of the year."

Charlie clicked his tongue, "You gonna have a git-together? Like ol' times."

Rhiney shook his head sullenly, now he was the one not looking up.

"Well- what'cha gonna do, then?"

Rhiney eventually met his glance, temporarily relieving Charlie (he thought Rhine was still mad about the bet), "I'm gonna do what all guys like me who are alone do. I'll try a few things here and there, find ways to pass the time. Then one day I'm off, sliding down that big on-ramp in the sky." He motioned his arm down, as if it were an amusement park roller coaster.

Charlie looked at him strangely, *this don't sound like no Rhiney I know. It's like he's an imposter.*

Then Rhiney began to laugh in that cock-eyed, teeth chattering way he always had. Charlie eventually joined him, only it hurt his face worse than ever. His laugh was wheezier on account of all the Reds. Rhiney used to smoke too, but quit about ten years ago. Meanwhile, Charlie was up to two packs a day, maybe two and a half since he took his little vacation.

They laughed until the waitress brought Rhiney his coffee, and Charlie his flapjacks and eggs. "Get me a coffee too," he growled out the corner of his mouth to her.

She sprang again like a jackrabbit, happy to get away from him and his table. Charlie chuckled in her general direction, but the laughter had been broken.

Rhiney took the toothpick from his mouth for a moment to sip his coffee. "Ahh," he murmured when he discovered it was too hot. Charlie began digging in, his two fists armed with a fork and a knife as he burrowed into his breakfast. Now, it was his breakfast companion's time to stare off into space. Rhiney looked off like he was pondering the most complex, personal question one could ever meditate on.

Meanwhile, Charlie ate as if he were starving for forty days and nights. He paid everything else no mind at all, until five minutes went by and his plate was clean enough to put back out at the buffet. He had been on his own so often, he genuinely forgot Rhiney was still sitting there. That was when he noticed him in his own, far-off world. Something in the back of Charlie's mind resonated, a distant voice calling out, *Maybe that shit he was saying before is what's eatin' Rhiney's old noodle. It's nothing you have to worry about though, Charlie. You ain't never gonna retire. No one ever looked in your portfolio and said, 'wow, let's pay this fine man to sit at home on his ass the rest of his rotten life.'*

No one will ever need anything from you. So why would they pay you for nothin'? Rhiney, on the other hand, he's an upstanding citizen compared to you. And you know what he's gotten away with in his career. Face it, Charlie. He's smarter than you. 10-4, good buddy?

Ya sleep in da bed you made, son.

"Hey Rhine," Charlie stared, vaguely aware that Rhiney *eventually* turned to his direction. "Stop me if ya heard this one," he chuckled, almost nervously, totally uncharacteristic of Charlie. "A guy's driving down the highway, a hot ass summer afternoon near Fort Worth. Him, and his pet parrot "Petey" beside him in the co-pilot. All 'the sudden, he sees a hot teenage girl on the side of the road. So he does the same thing we'd all do, Rhine. He pulls over, 'need a ride?' 'yeah.'" Charlie tried his best at a falsetto when doing the girl, he noticed Rhiney briefly chuckle when he paused to take a breath. Each time he did his voice came back louder and louder.

"And she climbed in the truck with only one thought on her mind, or so the driver thought. He moved his bird to the back by his bunk and after a couple of yardsticks down the road, he goes, 'You wanna go in the back and screw? Come on, babe. Let's make some fuckin' bacon!'"

Charlie's last line turned a few heads, he noticed Rhiney leaning back on his side of the booth, another strange trait that wasn't typical of the man. Still, something deep inside was making him tell the joke, only he didn't know what it was. He didn't even have to do anything; it just took control and did it for him.

"'Hell no!' the girl screams at him. 'Well, then get the fuck out.' So this guy pulls back over to the side of the road and does what we all would: he kicks her ass to the curb. So, a short while later, he's still kind of pissed off cause he was aching to give it"

nice and proper

"to her. He was watchin' her as he was drivin', she was maybe sixteen, but goin' on twenty-one in every sense. So he's driving along and it hits him, *no way can I be this fuckin' lucky*, he told hisself. He pulls over once again and there's standing another hot teenage girl! Again, he offers her a ride and again she accepts. This one looked even younger than the last one, and she was really slutty, just the way this guy like 'em. So a couple a yardsticks down, again he says 'Let's fuck! I'm gonna rock your world!' This one may have been younger, but she screamed louder than the last one did. But still calm, this guy says, 'no screw, no ride, bitch!'

"So again, he's off the road so quick he's skipping all kinds a gears. He's pissed again and starts to drive faster. An hour or so goes by and he can't even fuckin' believe his luck! Another hot teenage girl, this one a little older than the other two, maybe seventeen, and twice as hot and slutty, just the way he likes 'em. Down the road again he asks, straight this time, not being funny, 'Do you want to go in back and screw?' And she goes, 'yes!'

So he's thinkin', third time's a charm to hisself and all that. He finds a good spot in the middle of nowheres to pull over and leaves her in the cab for a second while he puts Petey in back with the cargo and digs a rubber outta his wallet. Then he goes to town on her. When they're done, another shocking thing comes outta her mouth. She goes 'I really don't need to go any farther, I'll just get out here.'

"This guy can't believe his luck. Not only was she a good fuck, but she wants to leave immediately after it's over. That'd be like a lot lizard throwing guys like us freebies, ya know? So he leaves her on the side of the road and pulls back onto it feeling good for the first time in a long time. But after a while this guy gets all soft and starts thinking maybe this girl would report him. Maybe it was one of them sting op-ah-rah-tions, and any time, they gonna trap him. Like my dad used to tell me, *the devil always gonna have luck on 'is side.* And sure enough, up come the cherries in the side mirror and the bear pulls him over. *Great*, he's thinkin' to himself, *she did fuckin' report me.* 'what's the problem, officer?' he asks the pig when he's down on the road talkin' to him.

"'no problem, man,' the cop says, 'it's just that your losin' your cargo out the back door. Just wanted to let you know, man.' 'SHIT!' the guy doesn't mind yelling in front of the cop."

Charlie took another pause when he noticed that half the diner and the waitress bringing him his coffee were all scowling in his general direction. It seemed to have made the waitress less timid, she firmly dropped it in front of him and hastily retreated. A few heads turned back to their respective positions, but a few remained, some shaking in genuine disapproval. "Fuck you," Charlie muttered loud enough for those closest to hear and turned to Rhiney.

His former companion stared back at him in that morbid curiosity again, but that didn't stop him from sinking down more and more in his seat, probably wishing that he hadn't accepted Charlie's invitation to breakfast.

Charlie noticed, but he didn't care. He didn't remember ever hearing this joke in one particular place. He figured that thing deep inside must have pieced it together from many jokes he heard fellas tell over the years on stops and on Sesame Street. All he knew was that he wanted to finish it.

"Anyway, Rhine. This cop follows the trucker to the back and what do they find? They find Petey, his parrot, throwing out the frozen chicken cargo that he was haulin'. And the bird was screeching at the top of its lungs, 'NO SCREW, NO RIDE! NO SCREW, NO RIDE!!'"

And that was all Charlie could get out. As much as his face broiled, feeling like the skin was melting off, he laughed his ass off. More faces of patrons turned back toward him and Rhiney merely kept his head down. Charlie paused to light a Red and slurp on his coffee, and then just kept on laughing– hardly noticing that Rhiney wasn't joining him at all.

After a loud and ruefully obnoxious coughing fit on account of his laughing, Charlie's sides began to numb and his face felt like it was on fire from his continuous sweating. He calmed himself by drawing large off his Red and slurping his java.

Rhiney finally looked up as the last few faces turned away again. His face was a mess of goosepimples, battered stubble and worn discolored cheeks. Which is to say, he almost looked as bad as Charlie. But he didn't look like that outside, as far as Charlie could tell he looked quite vigorous and raring to go.

"What's wrong wit'u, man?" Charlie asked, but was really thinking about getting to New Mexico before he went to sleep again. *Could go straight through and cut down through Vegas,* he thought earlier to himself. *But I hate them Western Colorado Rockies, everyone does.* Charlie would rather drive through the desert if it was at night. If he'd have been facing this choice driving in the daytime he probably would have opted for the mountains and go through Vegas at night.

Drivin' through them mountains at night is the safest way off a cliff.

Charlie thought of all this while his words hung in the air like the funnies in the paper. Like his dream. He gladly would have shared these thoughts with Rhiney, but he looked so sullen that even Charlie had to ask.

"Exactly what I said before," Rhiney subtly sneered. "That's what's wrong."

Charlie scoffed, not conveying the least bit of pity for him. "Shit man, I'll trade places with you, then. That's what's eatin' you? Shit! I'll ditch this load I'm carrying and me and you will go talk to the suits at Superfreight, then. We'll go in there and explain to 'em that you want to be-qehth me that retirement you got waitin' for ya at the end of the year. Shit man, I ain't gonna feel sorry for you no-how."

"You ain't heard the half of it."

"Out with it then, Rhine."

"Justine died bout six weeks ago," Rhiney uttered the tiniest of sniffs, but it was most likely due to a small cold. "I've just been thinkin' bout her a lot, you know. Just been thinkin' if maybe I'd still be with her, maybe she wouldn't a died. Ignorant stuff like that, you know. But I know it wouldn't make no difference. I know that."

"But Rhine, she was your ex-wife. Jeez! Smartest damn decision you ever made, if you ask me."

Rhiney stared at him questioningly, then his stare turned hard for a moment. Charlie thought he may actually get into one last brawl after all, that maybe he still wants his money from that damn bet. He cracked a knuckle in anticipation, but then Rhiney's look softened up again. Charlie's intention was not to piss him off, but to just sound off his beliefs. Of course, Rhiney had heard them all before, which was why he kept on talking.

"I thought so at the time, too. But I don't know. Maybe I'd want to retire if I was still with her. Maybe I wouldn't mind going home for good if she was there waitin' for me. There somethin' to that there, Charlie. You ain't never been married, so you don't know. There's something to that, all right."

Charlie held his breath, but when he finally exhaled he wasn't able to contain it. In his mind, Rhiney was talking absolute nonsense, and Charlie figured he could save him some embarrassment by setting him straight. If he would've kept his trap shut, Rhiney might have gone repeating that bullshit to some other people who would have thought Rhiney had gone bonkers.

It's the least I can do if I ain't gonna pay 'em for the Superbowl.

"Rhiney, I'm gonna tell you this to educate. That is the biggest crock a shit I ever heard. Let me tell you. Don't you 'member what life was like when you were married to her? She was a fuckin' bitch to you. That's why you worked all them goddamn hours, to stay away from that rag. That's the same reason Hal worked all them hours, so he could stay away from that sow he was married to. This is somethin' I ain't never understood about people. Your always fixin' to settle down just as soon as your dick goes limp for a girl. Then ten, twelve, twenty years down the line you can't stand the sight of 'em. Ya'll should have done what I did. I was the only smart one. Ya'll should have done what I did and you wouldn't have had to work them fuckin' hours."

As Charlie continued to blather on his focus changed from Rhiney to someone who wasn't Rhiney. It was like he was talking to himself, that no one was sitting in the booth across from him.

No one at all.

But of course, Rhiney was there. And Charlie was declaring his speech so triumphantly that it turned those same faces around once again. When Charlie finished, he glanced back to his old card buddy and was astounded by what he saw.

Rhiney was red with fury. An errant, hard tear was struggling to go back in the corner of his eye socket. He seethed at Charlie, so much so that a hot boiling gob of saliva sizzled as it landed on their table. "I'm gonna tell you one thing and then I'm gonna leave. You hear me, you old fuck? I don't give two shits about your life philosophies, but through good and bad, I loved Justine. She was the goddamn mother of my children and my best friend. Now I may've raked her over the coals with the rest of you fellas way back when, but that there was then, it's cause I was mad. I was mad at the whole situation back then. But don't get me wrong, Charlie. I loved her then and I love her now. And I ain't gonna sit here listening to you take a big old shit on the best times of my life.

"So from now on, Coldbrick, you ever see me at a stop or on the highway, just keep on going. Keep on truckin' till your outta my sight. Cause you never were a friend. A real friend don't sit there and say what you said to me. Don't matter what you think about life, if you was a friend you wouldn't of said that. So from here on out, don't talk to me, don't look at me, don't even think of my name. Whatever God has in store for you, that's up to him. I ain't gonna pray for you no more, Charlie. You on your own."

Rhiney stood up to leave, he glanced back down at his former friend one last time.

Charlie sat in the same position all throughout Rhiney's speech. Slowly, his face changed from awe to pure and utter blankness. When

Rhiney stood up, he continued to watch the space he sat in, as if he hadn't stood at all.

You sleep in da bed you made, son.

When Rhiney walked past him, he felt a cold wind flush by. It was the same wind he felt as a boy from the cellar door when his mother slammed it shut, locking him in the basement when she had a headache. Or when she was being mean. But this wind was like a breeze from Ontario in the middle of January. A sharp wind chill that burned his skin even more than the thing on his face. He was so remorseful, angry and embarrassed in that moment that the cornucopia of emotions, which Charlie was never able to handle real well, came back up the only way they knew how, in anger.

When the bell on the door rung shrilly, signifying that Rhiney was gone forever, Charlie squeezed his coffee cup in his hand until it turned purple and did his Nolan Ryan against the back wall of the diner. A few rebel beans slowly oozed down the wall in an explosion of hot Joe. A single scream from a woman in her thirties having brunch with her mother was the only sound that followed. Charlie turned beet red and felt his face split somewhere around his cheek.

Somewhere around that thing.

Slowly, blood petered out, but Charlie didn't notice until it plopped on the table. He looked around at the people staring at him in a surreal, white-hot horror. It's as if the last beams of the day's sun were blinding everything in the place as if a nuclear blast had gone off down the road. Charlie stole a napkin from the dispenser on his table and blotted his face gently, almost daintily.

He sneered at the diners on his way out, faces that looked on in hopelessness. For some reason, Charlie thought about how the patrons of the *Leatherneck* looked at the badass when he entered the bar. That sultry, static feeling in the air of a presence that is revered and feared. They watched Charlie go, some cowered or at least winced when he passed. They looked at him as if he were a monster, the thing on his cheek only adding to the spectacle. They looked at him as if he were Zeus or Goliath, ready to stomp on the tiny common folk for even the slightest infraction. He glanced at the waitress who was glad to eat their tab, just as long she never had to lay eyes on the likes of Charlie Coldbrick again.

The only sound heard in the place were that of Charlie's footsteps slowly ambling toward the door. Then the bell as he exited, heading back to his playground to burn off some of that steam that was boiling within him. He had done it now. Rhiney was the last one.

<u>16</u>

"Sleuth Stymie"

More dead ends greeted the detectives in the days following the interview with Abby at the hospital. It seemed like no matter which route they went, conventional or unconventional, some kind of force was working against them in figuring out this case. It was like a blanket or invisible veil that shielded their eyes by some kind of other power from the truth.

Several things had happened, although none of them substantial or meaningful to their progress. Detective Aspen finally broke down and went to see his physician, Doctor Remus, about the growth in his urinary tract. His partner understood why he needed to take a half day, but it still pissed him off. It was the day they were supposed to fly out to Sioux Falls, which delayed everything.

They had finally gotten a message from the district manager of Charlie's company out there, Tucker thought her name was Darla, but couldn't be sure. However, on the six separate occasions in which he tried phoning her back, at staggered times of the day, he was only greeted with an inane message machine.

The autopsy on Charlie's body was taking especially long. Favre, the medical examiner, came back with a preliminary result when he first examined the body: inconclusive. But every time afterwards they tried to phone him back for an update, they'd get the run-around– and once even a busy signal. On the day Aspen left early, Tucker ventured up to Globe himself to have a talk with him. The medical examiner was out sick that day, when he pressed the secretary, she admitted he went on vacation and should be back the following week. When Tucker questioned her why Charlie's body was sent to that district in the first place, he was only greeted with more flack and jurisdictional attitude by the county. That night, when Martha asked how work was, he confessed that he never really believed in God, but something was working against him and his partner in very mysterious ways.

There was also no word what-so-ever from the National Crime Database when they checked out Charlie's background.

Whoever this Coldbrick guy was, Tucker thought one day behind his desk, *he sure was slippery*.

They couldn't find one person who knew him, after exhaustively spending half an afternoon searching and calling nearly every Trucking industry in the southwestern United States. Nobody knew him and nobody wanted to suggest another route the detectives could take to find someone who did. Even a simple request to the Sioux Falls police department to search Charlie's apartment had apparently gone unanswered.

Aspen suggested one uneventful evening that maybe the water supply for the entire Sioux Falls area had fallen victim to radioactive waste. They shared another hearty laugh at that notion. It was a laugh not unlike the one at the hospital. The same admiration that was bringing them closer together was quite possible splitting the case apart. Each of them had silent mediations on that thought, although neither would admit it out loud. But a couple of days after Aspen had returned to work, he received a call from the forensics team– who were stationed in Globe. They were the individuals responsible for going over both of the vehicles involved with a fine-toothed comb. Aspen had known Bill Moss, the head of the team for years. They had met all the way back when they were both clerks for Judge Knoll at the county courthouse.

He answered the phone with a certain trepidation, wondering what bad news would come next, "This is Aspen."

Once Mr. Moss identified himself on the other end, Aspen shot up out of his seat so hard he grimaced at the left over urinary pain he was experiencing. The Cefadroxil Dr. Remus prescribed hadn't fully set in yet. "Yeah? What have you got Bill?"

Tucker, who was busy reviewing their files in the next room could sense the tone of urgency in his partner's voice and nearly tripped over himself running in.

Little by little, the stress waned from the Detectives voice as Bill, now the forensics man prattled on on the other end of the line. Eventually, he sat back down and began to slouch. That was until his voice was a mere whisper.

Meanwhile, Tucker took a seat across from his partner at his desk, folding his arms and resting his head, waiting patiently for the bad news. He hardly had time to shake his head dry of the white noise before he heard Aspen thanking Bill and hanging up the receiver.

Aspen stared straight ahead, fixated on some unknown or phantom object floating in the middle of his office. "Nothing. Only told me what we already know about the pickup, 'the seatbelt circuit didn't fail,' 'it was traveling approximately 70 mph,' 'the drive axel was different from the factory specifications indicating an extreme amount of force jolted the wheel from the vehicle. The truck was too old to have a diagnostic link connector, so it was impossible to tell what the actual speed was, or the engine speed, or the percentage of the throttle, or even if there was any activation in the brake system.' In other words, they got jack shit."

Tucker's eyes instantly filled with hurt and ferocity. Had his partner been looking at him, he may have thought a tear was welling up. But neither of the investigators had enough courage, stamina or intuition to even so much as acknowledge the other. Their world just seemed too cruel. It was unfair what was happening to them with this case, and there was no earthly justification for it. They were smart and they were capable, and this should have been open and shut. "And the rig?" Tucker asked after another moment filled with prickly pain.

"Nothing at all. They ran the VIN number and it was serviced at a DOT station in Iowa about a month ago. It was tip-top."

Tucker abruptly left his partner's office. A few moments later a loud crash could be heard from down the hall. Patience was wearing thin. The hammer above their heads was dangling by a thread. They both knew there was nothing left for them. They had milked Arizona dry for clues, at least at that moment. Perhaps their solace lied East in the vast wasteland of South Dakota. Whether it did or not, they were about to find out.

17

"A Remedy to Cure your Ails"

Charlie rode in silence down a lonely, bumpy stretch of I-25. His mind was still too numb to notice the passing multicolored wildflowers that lined the distance. Too many harsh, thundering echoes of words spoken in haste were swarming him to notice the many shades of green, meandering hills that followed. Forget about the rigid mountain shadows muting the vast open valleys, the large feather looking shapes ambling across the sky. He even passed a frigid, crystal lake that was so clear and so pure that it's a wonder if its contents were fit enough for man.

If he had been in a different frame of mind, he might have taken the time to enjoy the beauty of Southern Colorado; much like that little boy did years ago as he pissed and watched the moon.

But remote hours gave way to the night sky as Charlie rolled on down I-25, skirting the mountains as best he could. As Colorado Springs turned quickly to Pueblo, traffic started pooling up in the hammer lane. Tiny, red brake lights quickly followed as giant, towering lights flickered on as the sun flickered off. A road construction crew was hard at work paving the carved up lane, surrounding Charlie with a bunch of bored looking mountain folk, driving *Subarus* racked with canoes. They stared out their windows and peered into a dense mixture of humidity and tar smoke spewing from the workers' machines, dreaming of the coming winter where the streets and paths are paved with white gold.

But Charlie failed to notice this too, it didn't occur to him that he was still so numb with rage he had cranked the ten up to eighty as soon as the orange cones cleared. All he could do was focus on the words Rhiney had used and how he had used them. Part of Charlie wanted to hunt the prick down and drive him off the road, in those moments he tried hard to remember where it was Rhiney said he was going. But the only thing that jumped out in his mind was TEMPE.

By the time he arrived on the other side of Pueblo, heading toward Stern Beach, he calmed marginally. He still was plenty fired up, but he got to thinking that maybe he could have chosen his words more carefully. He was never about to lie to Rhiney, Charlie always prided himself on voicing his beliefs, but he could have been more articulate in his delivery of them.

Thoughts of the recent past still flooded his mind. He had been thinking about the trip, of how bad it had actually been.

If I wouldn't have taken that fuckin' vacation and lost my groove! his own voice screamed inside him.

If he had it to do over, Charlie never would have taken his vacation. For many kinds of reasons.

Some of which had nothing to do with the trip.

Charlie crumpled his cigarette pack when he pulled out the last Red as he maneuvered gracefully down a thirteen degree grade. The mountains weren't nearly as bad in Southern Colorado, but Charlie had to concentrate a bit harder on driving all the same. He had realized he hadn't performed one pre-trip inspection since he left Sioux Falls. It would've been fine if he were in the five, he had driven that thing nearly a million miles, he would know if something was wrong before any pre-trip. But the fact that the five was down in Florida and he was stuck out here with the monster ten made him slightly uneasy. But considering all the situations he had gotten himself in on this trip, he finally supposed forgetting was forgivable.

A few miles after he catapulted his Red out onto the side of the Wet Mountains, he abruptly decided he would stop in Colorado City for some more smokes, and perhaps a few other road supplies. Charlie figured he had nothing but misery on the trip anyhow, and he wanted– no– he *needed* to turn things around.

Nostalgically, he decided he would go back to what he used to do when he was having a bad time. He knew of a few choice areas to stop around the country. These are things you just pick up when you've been driving on the road as many years as Charlie had. He needed something to lift his spirits, and it was a particular something he hadn't had in quite some time.

<u>18</u>

"Pit Stop"

There wasn't a cloud in the night sky. It was a balmy fifty-five degrees as Charlie welcomed a light breeze that for once blew away from his face as he ambled into a Chevron station off the I-25 business route. It was eight at night, but Charlie figured it was Sunday on account that nobody was in the place but a gawky, teenage girl blowing a blue bubble that had imprints of the metal in her mouth.

Charlie grimaced at her, "Where's the can?"

She pointed toward the back by the fridges, she held Charlie's glance for a moment before looking back down to her magazine. He walked grudgingly toward it, almost as if he were limping. Still, his legs had already forgotten what happened in Council Bluffs a few days previous. He felt a little exhaustion, but chalked it up to too many hours behind the wheel, nothing Charlie couldn't handle, but enough for the DOT pigs to shred his hazmat until it was ribbons.

He pulled the chain on the overhead bulb in the seedy bathroom of the Chevron station. Graffiti was marked on every stained tile, everything from crude pornographic sketches to haikus. Charlie fixed himself up the best he could in the muted lighting scheme and the spotted mirror. He washed his hair in the sink and lathered his underarms with powdered deodorant. Anticipation was causing him to sweat slightly, so he took off the denim jacket. Other than his face, which could not be concealed without looking ridiculous, Charlie thought he looked the best that he could for an old timer. He wasn't tan anymore, those sunny days were long gone. And he wasn't as trim as he used to be, but he was still tough. He proved it to himself in Iowa, and he told himself that that was all he had left.

After an extra long piss, he grabbed a can of some unknown cola, bought a couple of packs of Reds and hit the road to the spot.

It was no longer a mandatory stop (mandatory to the DOT that is) on account that they gutted the scale and removed the information center. It now belonged to the drifters and second and third generation truckers who had passed the secret on to only the most proven and trustworthy. It was an even better spot because once it no longer became mandatory, the transportation department forgot all about it. It was merely a thin little strip of land in a low level valley. The street lamps haven't been replaced and the asphalt was as cracked as a horizontal highway hostess on pep pills.

19

"Horizontal Highway Harem"

Charlie slowed the ten to a rumbling halt in a rolling third, he actually killed it, but his mind concentrated on other things. Perhaps it was the fact that the place was now deserted, an empty shell of a lot off Route 165.

It was surrounded by looming Colorado pines and shielded between two peaks that reached upwards of ten thousand feet. A vacant looking shadow stood on the far side of the coop. Charlie could hardly make out its form, but soon remembered it was the utility shed.

It had clouded over somewhat– it felt to Charlie like a sprinkle was beginning to spit. But he could have just as easily been perspiring. He was a little nervous, but more let down because of the fact there was no human life that presented itself. It was something he imagined he'd never try again. But Charlie figured if pushed to the right limits, like he had been, a man could almost be persuaded to do anything according to circumstance.

He thought about environment once more.

Something else stood out too, that moving image in his head of Mrs. Juniper climbing into her lily white Galaxy all those years ago.

He sat in the ten, facing the highway, not a car had passed since he pulled in. Route 165 was like many of America's forgotten highways, it ran through a rough, rugged part of the country, and only three towns were attached to its windy hip. Colorado City, Rye and San Isabel.

He cracked a window, allowing the breeze to rush in and cure the air in the cab of burnt diesel fuel, tar from construction, and stale smoke from all the Reds. Charlie figured he would give it a little while, a few Reds at least. After all, it was still early, and lot lizards were a nocturnal breed.

After tossing another butt out the window, he pulled down a vanity mirror and wiped the dust off with the side of his palm. He touched the black bubble on his face, he did it gently, but it stung like a thousand killer bees. The thing was probably the size of a golf ball, it swelled and looked like it was ready to burst out of his skin. He sponged a tiny leakage in the corner with a napkin, it was where his skin split back at the diner.

"*Fuckin' vacation,*" he muttered softly to himself.

The rest of him looked in tact, but the thing on his face was on the right side. The side a potential passenger would be staring at. But it was a dark, nearly moonless night, and he finally settled that it would not be noticed.

Nervously, he drummed his fingers without any rhythm what so ever on the steering wheel. He took a last quick inventory of his wallet to make sure he had a love glove and at least thirty dollars – he had both. Scanning the area after his eyes had adjusted to the minimal lighting, he still only saw vauge shades of black and silhouettes of pine branches dancing flippantly in the gentle wind.

One hour and five Reds later Charlie still watched the darkness with acute interest. But after staring the same shadows in the eye for what seemed like a lot longer than an hour, his disposition had become glazed.

One car had passed since he arrived. It was a beat up old station wagon that was limping and clawing along the road like a wayward ant that had been stepped on, but can still move in aimless rapid movements. He had also heard the howl of either a wolf or some kind of mountain dog off in the distance. But that was it. The prime spot that Charlie and a select few others had held in such high regard was now a desolate wasteland.

He thumped his head lightly against the window his former friend had knocked on less than twenty four hours before. He was trying to conjure up the recollection of the last time he had visited this coop.

Five years?

Ten?

Time only seemed like a blur to Charlie. He contemplated setting up camp there tonight, but quickly thought the better of it. Even if he had found what he was looking for, he wouldn't have hung around long enough for his load to dry on the lizard's cavities.

It's true, he was ready and willing to take full advantage of their services, but he still viewed lot lizards and the crowd they ran with to be low-lives. Still, Charlie knew that he himself wasn't quite a model citizen either, but at least he was a workin' man. A vital element of the American machine – he was fulfilling his civic duty.

These card carrying whores only run with Gypsys, Mexicans, and Jews. I stick around and I'll get robbed of something or other. Assholes are always findin' ways to turn a buck.

All Charlie really wanted was what he *needed,* and he was prepared to cross into New Mexico tonight on the energy a fuck would give him. But it didn't look as if the opportunity would present itself.

A couple of Reds later, he checked his watch and was astounded to see that the midnight hour had come and gone thirteen minutes previous. He hadn't meant to stick around as long as he had, but his mind kept wandering to random subjects.

"FUCK!" he yelled in a gruff voice, as he pushed the ignition to fire up the ten.

It answered by rumbling to life beneath his feet, he let out the parking brake and let the tractor lurch forward. He hit the switch for the headlamps, they seemed to groan before they lit up. They shone heavily, piercing the darkness in an almost hazy complexion. He shouldn't have been able to see it, in fact, the DOT should have enforced his use of corrective lenses five years ago, but out the corner of Charlie's eye was movement in the darkness.

The utility shed door flipped open and out stepped a long legged lot lizard. She tried to walk with as much grace as she could, but stumbled twice and looked foolish. Charlie quickly cut the headlamps and his heart picked up a step or two. He had maneuvered his rig in a sort of angle that might piss off other drivers if they were to be stopping by for some action too. But he figured he would be fine since a clusterfuck wasn't in the immediate future of this coop. The air harshly spit out as he applied the parking brakes again. He decided to leave the engine running in case any gypsies were to jump out of the shadows. The last thing he did before the door creaked open and she joined him in the cab was check his breath against the back of his hand.

She crawled in, nearly falling twice. Abrasions and faded bruises were sprinkled across her face. Her arms and legs had the reminisce of a scab or two, but otherwise she would look to be in good shape to even the pickiest of customers. But one strike stood out to Charlie right off the bat.

A goddamn border jumper.

He sneered slightly, but then licked his lips and flashed a phony smile.

She was as thin as a rail, probably malnourishment from lack of food or excess of pills. Charlie knew that pimps this far South smuggled in cheap medication from Mexico and kept their lizards pumped full of pharmaceutical knock offs.

"High-ya honey," her voice whined smoothly enough.

She didn't sound as Mexican as she looked to Charlie. Somewhere inside, something in him shrugged. He could have gotten a toothless old hag who had been selling her ass since the Kennedy administration. The lizard was young, but her life had imprinted itself upon her hard already.

Besides, he thought, *a fuck's a fuck.*

"Hey," he grumbled because of a tar frog in his throat. Still, he was able to sound friendly.

"Sure do appreciate you comin' all the way out here tonight to visit me, baby," she wasted no time in caressing the side of his shoulder with a finger that was chilled, slowly working her way to his ear.

"I've been here for a while. I was fixin' to leave til I saw ya."

"Honey, I'm worth the wait."

These were the best kinds of women to Charlie. In and out, hello and goodbye – right down to the brass tact's of business. They'd shut up when they needed to and they worked fast enough to realize that both parties had things to move on to.

He smiled at her touch, relaxing both his heartbeat and his consistent sweating. Staring at her shadow in the night like that felt good, he just wanted to revel in it a bit. After all, Charlie thought that it might be the last fuck he ever gets. It didn't have to be mind-blowing, it didn't even have to be that good – it just had to be memorable. He fidgeted for his wallet and gripped it tightly in his hand. "How much?"

"Wha'cha got baby?"

He remembered seeing a dozen twenties in his pocket. Charlie wasn't much for banks, he preferred to keep his money where it would be safe – on him. He pitied the sap who would try and steal it from there– at least that is what he told himself. "All I gots is twenty bucks."

She sighed heavily, on the brink of boredom already, and they hadn't even got to business yet. "Well, that ain't enough for all of me, but I'll take care of you where you sit for twenty."

Charlie pretended to ponder this for a moment, he had every intention of accepting, but he liked to think of himself as a haggler. It also kept the lizard on her toes, he didn't want any woman to think he was a pushover. "Okay then," he said, waving a twenty at her after a few moments.

She grabbed it awkwardly and folded it into quarters, or so far as Charlie could tell in the shadows. She rolled it between her fingers and caressed it, as if she were checking to see if it was counterfeit. She faced Charlie and swayed her head around as if she were looking for something. "I can't see you," she huffed, this time with a thicker accent.

"You don't need to see nothin'," Charlie answered, sounding the slightest bit agitated.

"I want to see what you look like, man," she persisted.

"Are we doin' this or what, goddamnit! I've wasted enough time sittin' round here!"

"Usted es una policía?"

"I ain't a goddamn cop, lady!"

"Don't you want to see what I look like?"

"I don't care."

"I cannot see."

"Ain't you never heard of nocturnal vision?! Christ, I'm twice your age and I can see just fine! I thought *you people* would be used to seein' in the dark on account of skatin' 'cross the border so many times! Now are you gonna sit here and talk about the goddamn lightin' or are we gonna get down to business!"

"Hey! Fuck you, man!" her accent unfolded more and more. To Charlie, she begun to look more rigid– threatened– which in turn put him on edge. The air between them suddenly had become thick with tension.

Like a ball out of a cannon, like a cat pouncing on its prey, she frantically rustled around for something. Her hands searched the cab in a panic, as if she had been dying of a poisoning and Charlie had told her the antidote was hidden somewhere in the truck. First her hands ran among the cracked vinyl sun visors, and then along the middle as her rigid fingernails scrapped across the heating vents.

"Just what in the hell do you think you're doin'?" Charlie was more wound up by the noise she was making rather than her actions alone. His head throbbed when the conversation turned south and a jackhammer pounded away within his brain canal. And he never got headaches – not even the morning after a string of seven seven's.

She mumbled something in return, but due to her ever-thickening accent, Charlie thought he deciphered *turn the light on.* Her hands continued to search, but shied away from Charlie himself. She was afraid of him, that much was clear. It had saddened him a bit when he sensed it. With women he never tried to seem intimidating, he had just always come off that way – and he knew it. Her finger finally found the trigger to the dome light in the cab and she wasted no time pulling it.

A dim yellow light flashed on, causing the ugly situation to turn uglier. She wasn't as pretty with the light on as she had been in the shadows, which was part of the reason Charlie wanted it to remain dark. The other part was the inevitable look on her face when she caught her first glimpse of him. The thing on his cheek throbbed all the more, as if it were that faggy little banker back in Sioux Falls, it was just begging for its moment in the spotlight. The time for its fifteen minutes was right then and there.

The lizard stared for another moment and then her hands worked overtime. But this time it was in her own pockets, she was fishing out the carefully inspected twenty and tossing it back to Charlie. It fluttered down to his lap, like a helicopter on a landing pad. He stared at the face of a long dead president for a moment, until his attention was turned back to the lizard who started making intentions toward the door.

On impulse, or some other force inside him, he grabbed her arm with a mercenary, death like grip and stopped her cold in her tracks. She immediately tensed up and froze in his grasp, almost the way an animal would play dead to fool its predator. "What the fuck is going on?" he heard himself ask. "I thought we had a deal! This ain't no Mexican hat dance, bitch. When you make a business deal in America, you stay true to your goddamn word!"

He had not meant to do this – not at all.

This is not what he wanted.

This is not what he *needed*.

She weakly wriggled in his grip like a dried up worm on a fishhook, running on pure adrenaline and nerve. "I call Chulo! He's over there!" she pointed in a random direction, looking dazed and unsure of herself and her surroundings.

Charlie felt anger rising up in him, that same force that caused him to grab her arm. In that moment, he felt powerless to stop it. "You got a lot to learn about the real world, missy!" he shook her hard, causing her to stiffen again.

"I gave you the money! Suelta mi mano!" The longer he held onto her, the more and more frantic she became. She began to fight, slapping him with her free hand. After he still wouldn't let go, she spit at him.

That was all the longer Charlie could hold on to his reasoning, he drew back with ease and throttled his fist forward, making perfect contact with her petite face. He didn't give it his all, but enough for her to scream like the badass' minion who had gone soft in the middle of their battle at the *Leatherneck*. She screamed and cried, holding her face with the free hand as if she were under the ultimate tyranny.

Charlie blinked rapidly, he felt his whole body numb up like a seven seven buzz. For a moment, a fluttering of remorse crossed his path, but the anger came boiling back up and pulverized it. In another automatic movement, he pulled her closer to him so she would stop crying. "Listen to me! All I want to know –"

Her wailing started back up again, she was muttering more Spanish, she looked down when she did so, as if she were praying. He let go of her arm and grabbed hold of her hair, "Listen to me you fuckin' taco! Just tell me why you welshed on our deal…and I'll let you go!"

"I don't know what you say," her words calmed, but she still clasped her nose to stop it from bleeding – still distant and unfocused in the moment.

"Why do you come in here talkin' all sweet and turn me down?! What's WRONG WITH ME?!!!" he felt like he was asking the world, not just her.

No one will ever *need anything from you.*

She refused to answer him. Instead, her eyes remained tightly closed and she shook her head, repeating the universally known, "no, no, no, no, no" over and over again. The lids may have opened for the slightest of moments and gandered one last time at his face, but they quickly shut again as she continued to pray.

Charlie finally confirmed what he suspected all along.

She's discriminatin' against me in my own fuckin' country.

Instantly, his face turned sour. She no longer looked good to him at all. He was repulsed by the mere sight of her, and the fact that she was sitting in the same cab, the fact that she was sitting level and equal with him. He tried to stop himself, but the energy it took already had coursed its way through his nerves. In one smooth motion, he jimmied open the passenger door and gave her a violent shove. She fell awkwardly and hit the hard pavement four or five feet below. She groaned and screamed half heartedly, but sounded relieved at the same time.

"I hope you drown in the fuckin' Rio Grande when they ship you back, you diseased cunt!" he shot the words from his mouth like bullets from a gun.

She crawled a few paces, but was hurt bad enough to stop. The ten had been humming beneath their feet the entire time and Charlie figured it was as good a time as any to start crawling away himself. If she did have an entourage waiting for her back in the utility shed –

Charlie was still smart and sane enough to know when to retreat. And every tar filled molecule in his heaving body told him to get out of dodge right then and there.

<u>20</u>

"No Vacation goes Unpunished"

He revved the throttle as high as he could and worked the gears over something awful, but Charlie was back out onto Route 165 as fast as a trailer pulling half his weight. He neither heard, nor did he see anything else behind him. For all he knew, there were maybe three lizards or less back in that utility shed.

Coulda been just that one fuckin' moldy enchilada, he grimaced when he pictured her face again.

He wiped the sweat from his brow and rolled down the window to hawk one up and out. After, he lit a Red and turned the volume up on Sesame Street, hoping for a little background noise.

Something in him was stirring – that much was for sure. He decided he couldn't decipher if it felt better or worse than the thing on his face. It troubled him more than it should have. His heart refused to slow as he puffed arrantly on his Red, and stuffed the twenty the lizard threw at him back into his pocket. It had been a while since Charlie puked– or so he thought. He seemed to recall somewhere in the not-so-distant past that he had been this close or closer. He just couldn't remember when.

That was it for him.

They would have to put down those stop sticks and force the monster ten off the road to stop him from crossing into New Mexico. Although, some of the fury that had exhibited itself back at the empty coop had been replaced with something else, something Charlie hadn't felt since he was probably a little boy.

Oh come on, he whispered to himself.

The skin on his neck had turned bright red by the time he was back on the interstate. If he remembered correctly, Trinidad was a short hour or two drive from where he was, and New Mexico was not far behind.

I can do it, I'm not stopping for nothin'.

But something deep inside Charlie had disagreed with that notion. Something vile and earth rattling was bedding down in his intestinal region, and it throbbed. It almost cosmically answered Charlie's thought – and its answer was that it was going to make the ride to New Mexico as difficult as possible.

Charlie groaned when it did, even the thought of lighting another Red made him nauseous. He was going to have to grin and bear it for a couple of hours, he had driven under worse circumstances in the past.

Four hours – max, he told himself. *Colorado has to be ancient history... tonight. Oh and by the way* – a sudden realization occurred to him – *I'm quitting when I finish this here run. I'm ditchin' the ten down in*

TEMPE

Arizona, and I'll catch a flight back to Sioux Falls or Des Moines or Minneapolis if I have to. After that, I'm gonna march right into that upper office of 1609 Benson, and I'm gonna –

Charlie had enough fight left in him to stop that thought cold in its tracks. Deep down, near the throbbing, he was frightened to death of the rest of that thought. But as soon as his fear broached the notion, he instantly buried it as deep as it could go. Then, as if to antagonize him even further, his thoughts drifted back to the hard, meat packing sound of the lizard falling onto the pavement. That dry, hollow empty sound that he somehow was able to hear over the monster's growl. "Like I said –" Charlie spoke to no one in particular. *Colorado has to be ancient history...tonight.*

You sleep in da bed you made, son.

The troops Charlie enlisted to fight off the throbbing sensation in his stomach were losing ground. It had slipped into his throat and was on the brink of a catatonic, volcanic eruption. The sweat poured profusely from his scalp, it stung his eyes and burned the thing on his face at temperatures that rivaled Mercury. Charlie began to feel like he couldn't breathe, and he had only made it to Apache City. Any moment it was about to come out, but there was nothing he could do to stop it.

"No!" he screeched out, spittle flew every direction.

Please don't, his mind begged, tormented.

Little white flashes of light began to surface and fly out at Charlie in the granny lane of I-25. They hit the windshield and dissipated like shapeless blobs of life and landed back out onto the earth in a scorching pain that topped Charlie's.

10-4, HERE IT COMES! IT KNOWS YOUR 20! A voice screamed out of the jackhammer that continually pummeled the inside of his head, drawing ever nearer to the outside.

Charlie won only one battle with the force that throbbed in his throat and soon came out. He did not pull over, he kept on truckin' like the professional he deemed himself. As far as Charlie was concerned, in that last moment before that force presented itself, whatever else that happened inside the cab– *no one ever needs to know.*

It wasn't like he had anybody to tell anymore.

It didn't come out in the form he was expecting. Not the way he had felt in the not-so-distant past, or the way he felt when he was young, dumb and full of come, drinking fifteen seven-seven's in one night. It came out in that other form – the one he was deathly afraid of. The form that threatened any shred of dignity and self-worth that was still within his grasp. It was something else too.

That fuckin' vacation.

That one decision to take a few weeks off had cost him all the misery that accompanied him on this trip. Every rigmarole or curse he had run across all came back to that one thing.

That fuckin' vacation.

Charlie continued to drive, and somehow he thought he was doing an all right job in the moderate wind. It was creeping ever closer to one in the morning – mountain time. It was a good thing he had the road to himself, because he was soon driving down the middle, indicating ever more that this was his path – his playground. It was his access to his destination…New Mexico. He continued to amble down his path, and as he did, he did something he hadn't done since he was a little boy. Tears streamed down the battered face of Charlie Coldbrick. He cried.

Like all those times when his mother had been drinking and turned mean. Like all the times she hit him, or shoved him, or spit at him. He cried for all the times when he grew older and hit back. He cried for the time he cold-cocked his father when he found him with another woman. He cried for that fuckin' lot lizard back at the coop he had fled. He cried for Rhiney because he had severed the thin string that held together their friendship. He cried for that thing that was rotting his face to the promise land. But most of all, Charlie cried because he thought of the last time he really did vomit, and it turned out to be not that long ago at all.

That fuckin' vacation.

<u>21</u>

"Now the Time has Come"

Charlie ambled through the door of a fairly new strip mall on the top of Cliff Hill– just east of the Sioux Falls International Airport. The door had a thin metal rail for a handle, and it squeaked like a mouse under Charlie's boot as he opened it. The faint smell of plastic, sterilized medicine turned to an all out waft as he approached the receptionist's desk. She was a moderately built woman in her fifties, too many years away from retirement to be completely indifferent about her job duties, but enough seasons under her belt to hold all the power. Charlie disliked her immediately.

But sure enough, he approached the desk, dragging with him the stink of last night's seven-seven binge. "I'm Charlie Coldbrick," he croaked. The many Reds he smoked out front, trying to work up enough nerve to go inside, protruded from his foul breath. "I had an appointment at 10:00."

The receptionist glared out at him behind her large, steel rimmed glasses. She glanced back at the clock on the wall, purposely, to illustrate her point. The clock indicated that it was 11:04. She glanced at the appointment book briefly and passed him a clipboard with enough forms to keep him busy for a while, along with a bright, yellow ballpoint pen. "I need to make a copy of your med card," she groaned impatiently.

She returned at once and instructed him to sit, *it may be a while.*

He couldn't fight off the compulsion to mumble back, *I'm sure it will.* As Charlie tried to remember the intricate details of his medical history, because it had been many years since he saw a doctor, he surveyed the waiting room. There was an old lady with a brightly colored silk scarf wrapped around her head, her skin was frail, but smooth as butter. She sat under a TV displaying a mid-morning talk show, but stared at a little bald boy of about three, playing with a set of *Lincoln Logs* that were left out for children. A few elderly men were scattered throughout the rest of the rows of uncomfortable chairs, padded with an ugly turquoise color. One man peered through his cheater's glasses as he mumbled softly to himself, filling out his form.

The little boy's mother was behind Charlie in line and sat three chairs away, too close for Charlie's comfort. He slyly studied her as she glanced back and forth between her forms and her son, working out in his head what type of woman she was.

Probably drivin' some bran'ew Camaro with leather seats and a car phone, weaving in an' outta traffic, with her poor-bastard-of-a-son bouncin' 'round in the back seat. Her husband's probably a lawyer, workin' overtime in his office downtown, fuckin' his sec-reh-tahry and thinkin' bout how he can leave his wife with more than the clothes on his back. The whole thing's a goddamn vicious cycle.

When Charlie went off on his mental tour, he came back just in time to see the woman looking at him – for some reason, she was smiling at him. It caught him completely off guard, so he widened his face, his best attempt at a smile, and quickly darted his eyes back on his own paper.

Long after he was finished filling out his forms, he had begun watching a talk show that featured guests who were considering transsexual surgery. Charlie watched with anger, scowling all the way. Two of the three elderly men had already gone in ahead of him, as did the mother and her little boy. He had got up once to take a piss, and two other times: one to simply pace because he was in dire need of a Red. The other to bitch out the receptionist who remained calm. She gave him a lame sort of runaround, *your doctor is still on the road coming in. AND WHEN HE GETS HERE MR. COLDBRICK, you will be the second person to know.*

When Charlie tried to inquire further, asking for an ETA, she simply pointed behind and beyond him, instructing him to sit down. And for some strange reason, Charlie obeyed. At the very least he distanced himself from her area. She had one of the few qualities in a woman that made Charlie listen to her. He scratched his face and tried to figure out what it was. *Must be because she's so goddamn*

mean

bitchy.

He paced the room faster and faster. He stopped only to take a sip out of the drinking fountain to calm his nerves and fight off the urge to step outside and smoke all the Reds at his disposal. The craving was so fierce it flared up the goose pimples that were beginning to form on his cheek. They had popped up several weeks ago. At first he thought he shaved wrong and caused a couple of ingrown hairs. Then he thought it possible to be a couple of whiteheads that sprouted up, mistaking his flesh for that of a scrawny, gawky teenager. But when the imperfections began to harden and root themselves in his second and even third layers of skin, that's when Charlie decided to see a doctor. He even took a couple of week's vacation from work, because lord knows he had no other use for it.

The urge had boiled over and at the beginning of Charlie's leap into the air, he intended on taking down all of his Reds – every last single one of them. But mid-leap, the receptionist's long, hollow voice called out his name, "Coldbrick!" as if she were a warden taking roll call in a prison. His mind longed for the cigarette, but his feet overrode and steered him toward the desk. Standing behind the receptionist was a tall, skinny guy with a long cashmere jacket and a plad scarf that stood out like a sore thumb in the middle of summer.

He stuck out a hairy hand to greet Charlie while awkwardly adjusting his wire rimmed glasses with his other. "Mr. Coldbrick, I'm Dr. Cassock, we spoke on the phone a couple of days ago."

Charlie's tension began to mount, but he refused to show it to the preppy little twerp that was two weeks out of med school. "Yeah, what's up, doc?"

Dr. Cassock sniggered genuinely enough, he wasn't quite old enough to scoff at that particular comment, which is no doubt thrusted at thousands of doctors across the land upon first meeting. "Well, sorry I'm late Mr. Coldbrick. I was happy to hear you were a little tardy as well. This fine young lady will show you into a room and I'll be along in a minute. I have to get myself situated. Then we'll have a little talk. Sound ok?"

"Sure. Whatever."

The young doctor responded with the same abrupt, stifled laugh that even the receptionist glanced over at him questioningly.

<u>22</u>

"Me No Fry: Ain't Gotta Worry No More"

As Charlie waited, he glanced around the room. He hadn't sat like that in a doctor's office for at least thirty years – if ever. Charts and banners were littered across the wall like it was a college dorm room instead of an examination room. Glass jars filled with cotton balls, wooden popsicle looking sticks and hypodermic needles were sprawled across a small desk in the corner. Parked underneath it was a backless swivel chair on wheels that shined silvery in the mild lighting scheme. There was a vinyl mat perched on top of an examination table that sat higher than anything else in the room – like a throne – Charlie figured it was for pregnant women on account that it had feet hooks on the end of it.

A poster that hung above the sanitary station immediately caught Charlie's eye. It featured a blazing, ugly red background with thunderstrikes of golden yellow and fiery orange thrown in for good measure. Right in the center of the poster was a picture of a sun which (was supposed to indicate, although Charlie didn't think it was doing a very good job) was purely evil. The sun had a contemptuous, yet arrogant grin strewn across its face. The caption below read in big, black bold lettering: DONATE TO AUSTRALIA'S LEADING CANCER PREVENTION PROGRAM, "ME NO FRY." Below the bold letters sat a perfectly content and confident cartoon man, lying in a lounge chair by the pool. He sizzled with his flawless, golden, healthy skin. He had a pair of blue, pointy shades on, and bared his teeth right back up at the sun who was glancing down on him. Charlie stared at it, wondering what the hell the picture had to do with fighting cancer.

But a clattering sound of the door opening and Dr. Cassock walking in fit with a neatly pressed lab coat and a wide smile on his face distracted him. "Charlie, sorry to keep you waiting," his smile actually widened as he spoke, his gums and lips white from the pressure. He sat down in the swivel chair and placed a metal folder of Charlie's forms on his lap. "How are you feeling today?"

Charlie, wanting to get out of the building and be rolling down Cliff hill as soon as possible, cut right to the chase. "My face itches and I got these fuckin' hard bumps that won't go away. I figured they were cysts at first, but they're getting hard as a rock. I can feel it growing under my skin too. I think they changin' color." He winced, he surprised even himself that he was able to accurately describe his symptoms in such an expressive manner (for Charlie that is).

"I understand," he nodded as he opened the folder and skimmed through Charlie's medical notes more thoroughly. "Sorry, I just got here from Rochester and I've barely had time to read this. Let me – just real quick." He began reading at a frantic, but smooth pace. He was nowhere near the wreck Charlie was at the moment.

Charlie felt very uncomfortable sitting in a place where he couldn't have a Red. His heart paced, but was on the verge of accelerating. The air conditioning was humming along nicely through the ducts, but sweat trickled and glimmered in the light through the thinner areas of his scalp.

"Okay, it says here that you saw Dr. Xiong. A resident doctor here a couple of days ago?"

"Yeah, I saw that guy," Charlie remembered to himself.

Little nip didn't tell me shit. All he did was quote a bunch of medical terms that I could barely understand through his goddamn yellow mush mouth.

"Yeah, he didn't tell me shit. He was what you might call, evasive. See? I can use smart words too. The little bit I could understand was about seeing a specialist. Well, I guess that's you. Why don't you tell me why I have to be here talking to you today, instead of at home sleeping it off?" Charlie felt weak, he hadn't eaten in several hours, and it was the absolute longest he had gone without a Red since he was a teenager back in school.

Dr. Cassock nodded through Charlie's rant. It appeared he hadn't even been listening. The smile had disappeared from his face, but he was focusing intensely on Charlie's file. Even when Charlie stopped speaking he continued to nod slowly. But then he surprised him by snapping the folder shut again and looking Charlie in the eye, still not smiling.

"I just want to take a look here." He reached into the black medical kit he had placed on the table and produced a vertical scope with a lens and a flash bulb in the middle. He stood up and instructed Charlie to look up and point his cheek to the sky. Studying it under the lens, he murmured something and sat back down, placing the instrument back onto the table.

"You too, huh? Man, I shoulda been a doctor. Get paid a hundred grand a year to sit there and make noises."

"Now, now, Mr. Coldbrick. I can assure you, I don't make a hundred grand a year."

"You will soon enough," Charlie muttered, dumbstruck that the doctor even acknowledged the comment. For some reason, it proved to be an admirable gesture to Charlie. It made him like the doctor a little bit.

Dr. Cassock smiled briefly, sensing he was able to break the ice with him, "I come from a family of doctors. Every one of us has a license to practice medicine. I guess I was just born into it."

"How *nice*," Charlie retorted back to his usual, nasty self.

"Mr. Coldbrick, I promise I will explain all of this. I will not be evasive and I will make sure everything is crystal clear, okay? I just have to make sure of something before I do that. I need to excuse myself for just a moment, but I'll be right back." He wagged his finger randomly through the air, to authenticate his promise.

By the time he returned, a tiny puddle of salty sweat laid at Charlie's feet. At that moment, Charlie felt like he could have snapped the good doctor's neck in half. He was completely jittery, shaking so bad it looked like an electrical current was coursing its way through his bloodstream at a steady pace. Dr. Cassock noticed the sweat dripping like icicles in the sun off of Charlie's sopped head. It took him a moment to react though, the smile erased from his face.

"Sorry to have kept you waiting, Mr. Coldbrick. Oh my gosh, I'm sorry, I'll turn up the air conditioning." The apologetic doctor pranced over to the thermostat on the wall and nudged it down to a more tolerable temperature.

Charlie hardly noticed any of it. His mouth quivered in vibrations, aching for a Red, his chest was about to explode and the queasy feeling he had had in his stomach returned ten-fold. He glanced at the doctor through glassy, tear-filled-just-about-ready-to-burst-wide-open eyes. What he saw hadn't reassured him. The misty, painful look in the good doctor's eyes downright terrorized him.

It also seemed that the Morse code of tension buzzing through the air was sensed by Dr. Cassock as well, he hesitantly reclaimed his seat in the swivel chair and groaned as he sat.

"Well, doc," Charlie was barely able to keep his voice from shaking. "Did you find out anything useful for me?"

"Mr. Coldbrick-" croaked the doctor, who stopped to clear his throat. He turned red from embarrassment, caused by the meandering sound he made. As if he were some pubescent boy whose voice was changing.

To keep his sanity in check, and to delay the news he always knew was in the back of his mind, no matter how many weeks he ignored it for, Charlie answered, "Christ doc, I knew you were young, but shit –"

They shared a nervous giggle that didn't even begin to curb the apprehension that was thickening.

"Mr. Coldbrick, I was called in from the Mayo Clinic, in Rochester –" he paused to clear his throat once more. "What I mean to say is – more specifically – I was called in by Dr. Xiong after he examined you on your last visit. Dr. Xiong called me in because of my expertise in the field. You see, I was just talking to Dr. Xiong and cross referencing the results of our individual examinations of you, Mr. Coldbrick. We have to run a few tests to be 100% positive, but there is a large chance that the legions on your face is a result of melanoma cancer cells." He paused, maybe to see if Charlie had any sort of reaction to his news.

Charlie not only remained silent, but inside he felt serenely calmer. He thought the doctor may have thought he hadn't heard him – or refused to. All of his terrified symptoms from before remained, but in an almost controlled environment. Yet somehow, Charlie felt it may have been the calm before the storm.

"We base this diagnosis on the fact that the lesions on your face are forming into one, they've become particularly hard as you stated before. And they're spreading laterally across your skin. The fact that you said it felt like they were growing underneath is troublesome. If that is true, then soon the lesions will take on a dome shape and start to grow and puff out. This, unfortunately indicates that the cancer is at its latter stages. If all this proves to be correct, Mr. Coldbrick, and Dr. Xiong and I concur that it will be, we need to remove the lesion right away. The sooner we get to removing it, the better chance the cells have of regenerating and..." the young doctor stammered, "the better chance we have of extending your life."

Charlie finally acknowledged the doctor's words, "*Extending*, huh?"

Dr. Cassock nodded, "Like I said, we'll have to run some tests, but we fear that this is something that has been going on for a while. Mr. Coldbrick, have you had many extended periods of exposure to the sun in the last twenty years?"

Strangely, or so the doctor probably thought, Charlie started to laugh. It was no longer a nervous giggling like the fit he and the doctor had shared a few moments earlier, it was full on side-splitting laughter. The kind he and Rhiney and some of the other fellas used to share over their full-houses and straight-flushes all those years ago. It was the kind of laughter you could only share with your favorite people in the world.

As Charlie wheezed and coughed, his mind screamed for another Red. The doctor finally interjected loudly with, "Mr. Coldbrick, I can appreciate that this news may come as a shock. I can also recommend a good psychotherapist that helps people like you deal with news like this."

Eventually, Charlie was able to regain control of his coughing fit, he scoffed and looked up contemptuously at the doctor. The bile in his stomach was beginning to rise, and he decided it would blow like Mt. Crackatoa if he didn't get out of there ASAP.

Besides, Charlie thought, *I learned all I need to know here.*

"I ain't going to no head shrinker, and I certainly ain't goin' under the knife."

"Mr. Coldbrick, you must realize this is serious, and it could end up taking your li –"

"Do you know why I just had that there fit? Why I carried on when you ask me if I spent much time in the sun?"

"No, Mr. Coldbrick. Why?"

"Cause you obviously ain't heard what I do for a livin'."

"No, I never learned your occupation."

"I'm a goddamned truck driver."

"Did you ever use protective lotion for your skin?"

"No, I sure didn't."

"Look, we don't have to do this now. I need to schedule an appointment with you again, before we go ahead with surgery."

"I already told you, there ain't gonna be no surgery."

"Mr. Coldbrick you're not in the right frame of mind right now. Why don't we do the tests first and then we ca –"

"Don't call me crazy, doc. Not if you ain't a head shrinker. Bottom line, there ain't gonna be no surgery. I can't afford it. I'm paying outta my own pocket just coming here to learn what I've learned. I ain't got no medical insurance, never chose to have it. My company is this close to canning my ass anyhow. I'm down to my last strike just taking these here four weeks off so I could get this shit straightened out. Well, I came here and found out what I needed to find. I can't afford to take no more time off work. In two weeks, I gotta go back. I can't afford it neither, not the way things are. It just ain't in the cards for me, doc."

The doctor sighed patiently, maybe slightly amused, but certainly he wasn't smiling at the stubbornness Charlie portrayed. "I don't think you realize the severity of the situation Mr. Coldbrick. If you do nothing about this, things will not be easy for you in the immediate future. And if you are talking about returning to work, that would mean more exposure to the sun, that would only speed up the spreading of the cancer. You will also experience a whole array of unpleasant symptoms like: headaches, fatigue, weight loss and bone pain depending on where it spreads. It is too close to your lymph noids, if it spreads there it will be extremely painful and then we would have to look into chemotherapy.

"Now, if cost is an issue, naturally there are programs for people in your situation."

"I'm sorry, doc. I have to go back to work." Charlie said, almost in a chipper tone.

For the first time, the doctor looked frustrated and panic-striken all at once. "Mr. Coldbrick, you will die a very painful and horrible death."

"Well, I ain't gonna spend my last days on earth lying in some fuckin' hospital bed wrapped in bandages like a fuckin' leper so you can help me die *better*." Charlie stood up quickly, the doctor flinched like he was about to pop him one. "Relax, I'm leaving. You ain't gotta worry about me no more."

As Charlie stood up, white noise flowed into his ears from some unknown source. It was a slow leak at first, but it soon was faster and faster.

He faintly heard the doctor's voice registering in higher, more frantic octaves as he made his way back toward the lobby, but he paid them no mind. Too many images were flashing through his mind. The world seemed to move in slow motion around him, as if the gravitational pull on earth had just shifted dramatically.

When he arrived out in the waiting room, the sun was beaming brightly through the flat windowpanes. For a moment, all Charlie saw was white, but slowly his retinas cooled and things came back into focus. When they did, Charlie was staring down at a pile of his own vomit in the foreground of a shallow, shiny metal tub with holes like a noodle strainer in the bottom for a drain.

When he glanced up and wiped at his orange stained mouth, he saw the receptionist's face contorting in drastic movements. She was yelling loudly at him; he had just puked in the drinking fountain, but the white noise prevented anything above a hundred decibels from traveling into his ear.

Dr. Cassock appeared behind her in the hallway, his face white as a ghost, his posture stiff and awkward. They, along with a couple of women in their thirties dressed in spandex jogging suits stared at Charlie. He looked them all over once and headed for the door. He still walked in slow motion until his hand touched what it had been rummaging his pocket for, the half pack of Reds he put there before he came in.

Outside, he lit it and an instant wave of relief washed over him. He let the cool afternoon breeze from the west blow across him as he puffed and itched his face. It almost made him forget about everything that had happened in there. The only thing that crossed his mind as the white noise slowly drained from his ears, was how he was going to spend the rest of what would inevitably be the last vacation he ever took.

<u>23</u>

"A Flash Before Your Eyes"

A large jolt under the belly of the tractor shook the cab enough for Charlie to awaken from his visit to the recent past. It snapped him out of whatever mystical spell the shimmery interstate had cast, as it tends to do. It turned out to be nothing more than a change in the bedding of the road. All eighteen wheels that Charlie commanded at will, like a general steering a chariot in some grand, ancient battle, kissed smooth, cool, freshly laid tar. The mechanical popping noise one normally gets in a car's wheel-wells was nonexistent over the roar of the diesel engine droning in tenth gear.

Charlie was astounded to find himself still on the road.

How many goddamn minutes was I out?

He patted and goosed himself frantically with his free hand, checking to make sure that he was in one piece. He checked the mirrors and peeked at the exterior of the ten, even under the dimly lit marker lights, he could tell it was fit as a fiddle. Charlie instantly wondered if his luck was possibly changing. A small part of him saw the light of day for the first time in years: the hopeful part. He scanned the road like a cat, feeling completely in tune and aware of any and every thing around him. His little spell, or whatever it was, seemed to have sharpened his senses.

Charlie thought of it the same way as when you take a power nap. Sometimes that one half hour can make you feel like it had been an entire night and day. Where if you were to sleep that long, you feel completely lethargic when you awaken.

But that was exactly his trouble; he had no way of telling how long it had been. He also couldn't remember the last town he had passed before he slipped into his tunnel. He closed his eyes and tried to picture the road sign. God knows he wouldn't have to use his imagination for that. He had seen his share out on his playground to say the least. He knew it was green, and the lettering was white. But when the lettering came into focus, the only thing it read was TEMPE.

The last thing that Charlie remembered was throwing the lot lizard out onto the pavement and the dull, meatpacking thud that followed. Everything after that had dissolved, lost at the speed of a diminishing dream in the deepest slumber.

But Charlie couldn't accept that, he considered himself a logical person, even if his mind *had* begun to slip. He continued to search for clues while monitoring the road, anything that would determine how much time had passed. It was still dark outside, so that didn't reveal anything. He checked the mileage on the tractor, but then realized he couldn't remember the last time he checked, if he even checked at all.

He still thought he was in the mountains. It was dark, but little ridges and shapes that may have resembled Colorado pine branches poked out of the darkness. Then, a bright green sign beside the road was zooming towards him. Charlie finally uncoiled because that meant it was directional information or mileage, something that would tell him where he was.

One thing did creep back to Charlie from the last who-knows-how-many hours.

Colorado has to be ancient history…tonight.

The signed loomed large atop of two posts, written in loud, uber-bright script: **RANTON PASS, ELEV 7,834 ft.**

Charlie had done it.

He didn't know how, but he did it all right. Ranton was the first town worth noting when crossing into New Mexico via I-25. It was no Sante Fe or Albuquerque – or even a Las Vegas for that matter. But still, it was a good twenty miles into the state.

Somehow, he had done it.

He lit a Red to celebrate as the blood streamed smoother through his veins, revitalizing him. He eventually even forgot about the thing on his face. It had clouded over into a dull, gray dome that trickled faint blood and ooze he didn't want to imagine, let alone touch. Charlie Coldbrick felt so good that he accomplished his recently rediscovered mission that he was prepared to take a break, maybe a long one.

Wait till midday, till the goddamn glorious sun is high on the horizon. By the time I get to the desert, it'll be fixin' to set.

He decided he would stay in Ranton, maybe even get a motel.

He earned it.

He *needed* it.

<u>24</u>

"Halfway Between the Gutter and the Stars"

The stiffness in his back cried out like a child with a skinned knee as Charlie stretched from a long, well-deserved sleep. Out of necessity, and of course old habit, he reached for the pack of Reds he left lying on the bedside table constructed of cheap scraps of plywood. Also out of old habit, he glanced at the clock. Something had sunk in and dissipated over the last fifteen hours of sleep. The giddiness of making it into New Mexico that accompanied him the previous day was long gone and out of sight. All that was left was Charlie.

Late last night, Charlie checked himself into the Starlight Motel, just off route 72. He'd been there before a few times, back in the old days. But because of his late arrival at the Starlight, he had almost completely slept through the day. He wrapped his complimentary comforter around himself, it was brisk because he left the air conditioner on high. With one strong whip of his arm, he threw open the dusty drapes.

The sun was absent out Charlie's stained motel window, all that remained were sharp shadows in the parking lot, and wavy grassland with mountains in the distance. Up above, translucent, conditionless skies with large, weightless feathers migrating across it seemed to wink at Charlie as he peered.

Must be facing east, he thought softly to himself as he choked his inaugural Red.

Charlie, for the briefest of moments, entertained the notion that it was the end of a second day, but quickly dismissed it. Although, it wouldn't have surprised him, his sleeping schedule had been erratic at best ever since

that fuckin' vacation

he came to work. It felt like he had been back for months, but then he remembered that it was still his first trip.

TEMPE.

Charlie dropped the blanket and let the continuous artificial air bathe his heaving and diminishing body. The brazen pride he had always associated with his work ethic had been lost from these last few – *what? Days? Weeks? Months?* Charlie knew where he was, but had no idea the day of the week. He knew he left Sioux Falls sometime in August, probably somewhere in the middle– the 20th at the latest.

Normally, he would just check his log, but something told Charlie he hadn't followed the DOT pig regulations closely enough. He knew it had taken him forever and a day just to get to Nebraska. But how long had he been traveling since then?

If it were Hal he was driving for, he would have called ages ago. But why hadn't Darla the dyke contacted him on his Qualcom? Charlie never had too many people call to check on him when he went to work, but usually he would receive something. Either from the company he was driving for, or the terminal that was expecting the shipment. But for the first time on his self proclaimed cursed trip, he realized no one had tried to contact him at all.

This briefly made him think that maybe that much time hadn't passed after all, but something in the realm of time passage had still not settled right. Quick thinking, he picked up the cream colored handset off the cradle of his complimentary telephone, and dialed "0".

"Front desk," the labored, disinterested voice on the other end answered.

"Hi, front desk, hiya – this is room #117, I need to uh – request a wake up call- for tomorrow morning. Yeah."

A sinister silence greeted Charlie's fumbling words, and for a moment, a chill went down his spine that isolated him even further. But then the voice returned from whatever space time continuum it had retreated,

"And for what time would you like this wake up call, sir?" the voice sighed, more impartial than ever.

Charlie choked on a hacking cough he wasn't sure would end in time to keep the operator on the phone. But he was able to spit up a large piece of his inner lung and clear his throat to ask, "Well, let's see – what day is it now?"

"It's Tuesday afternoon, sir. Wait a minute – Did you say room #117?"

"That's right," his voice wheezed and winded into the telephone.

"I don't see you anywhere on the guestbook, when did you check in?" His voice rose slightly. No longer did the front desk sound blasé about what he had to say. A sense of urgency had surfaced in the operator's voice, and it didn't sit well with Charlie one bit. It only added to the edginess he'd been feeling since he awoke.

"I checked in –" He stayed silent for another period, "Christ, it must have been last night. It couldn't have been – yeah, it was round last night."

"Okay, Darnell must've been neglecting his post. He wasn't supposed to rent that room out to anyone yet," the front deskman sounded as if he were reciting the rules to himself rather than Charlie – just to keep everything straight. "For how long would you like to keep your reservation? Through tomorrow?"

"How long do you need me?" Charlie's voice was hardly above a whisper.

"What?"

"I mean – Tuesday, yeah. It's Tuesday. I know that. But what's the date?"

"It's the 16th of September, sir," the operator sighed impatiently, his apathy returning to him.

A faint tugging swiftly pulled the strings of Charlie's heart, but it disappeared just as quickly. He had been expecting something like this. He had been out on this playground of his for far too long. But it made it all the more curious as to why Darla the dyke had completely ignored him. She didn't like him – of course – not too many people who had met Charlie Coldbrick did. But one would think she would like to know where her tractor was.

"Sir?" the voice on the other end called out to Charlie.

"Oh, yeah. You know, uh – cancel that wake up call. But- uh- yeah- I'll be checking out today. I've got to go. I'm leaving right now." He slammed the receiver down on its cradle, but it wasn't too long before he picked it back up again and worked over the rotary mechanism frantically. He, in turn, didn't care all that much for Darla either.

But your work is your work, his old ethic cried out.

The ominous ringing on the other end only pushed Charlie deeper and deeper into his dark tunnel. This 5:00 pm morning had become too strange for him, and it began to piss him off plenty. After eight rings, something mechanical clicked on the line, Charlie was about to croak out Darla's name, but a message had come on in her uninhibited, masculine voice:

"Hiya, you've reached Pioneer Trucking inc., the fastest freight in Sioux Falls. We are unable to take your call right now, cause it's past quittin' time, or we're out in the yard. Either way, leave us a message and we'll call you –"

He slammed the receiver down even harder than before. So much so that the walls shook and the earth groaned.

How could this of happened? he wondered.

But of course, there was no one around to answer. There was only Charlie– in his dilapidated motel room that stunk of moldy paint and even moldier ghosts. Suddenly, he felt a sharp pain stab him on the tip of his cheek. His skin was splitting again.

"Fuck!" he cried out of frustration as he waywardly wandered naked, except for his shorts, over to the chipped bathroom mirror. The thing on his face, or the lesion, as that dimestore doctor referred to it as, had popped. The ends had come undone, and it had split right down the middle at the seams, much like Charlie's ability to handle the insight he had recently gained.

Perhaps out of catatonic despair, he viciously eyed his buck knife on the bedside table drawer. He imagined all the things he could do with it. With that tool, he could very well do anything he wanted. He could perform his own goddamn surgery and cut that thing right out of his face. Or he could simply aim lower and slit the vital vein in his wrist.

Maybe I could just stick it into my guts and give her a good twist, he dreamed dazedly.

He also thought about exacting all of his revenge on the world by taking the front desk clerk hostage and rattle off all of his uninhibited, cantankerous demands of the world through the phone the pigs throw through his window.

He glanced at himself in the mirror again, blood flowed intermittently down his face, as if a spigot had been pumping it instead of his heart. Looking frail and sunken, Charlie felt his age for the first time ever. He was not the same asshole that had mopped up the floor with the badass and his cronies a few weeks ago in Council Bluffs.

No.

What stared back at Charlie in the mirror was a deflated human being that for the first time may have realized his whole life had been constructed of a lie. Charlie was no dummy, he knew that we all lie to ourselves to be happy, but there are fewer of us that spin in such a way that we come to depend on it.

We come to *need* it.

As he dabbed daintily at that result of his years of neglect, not just of himself, but of the world he lived in, he was cooling on the inside. Charlie realized something in that moment: the doctor was right about one thing. He wouldn't be able to do his job anymore.

Can't work like this, his mind grimaced at him.

Before the blood clotted and he packed up his things to get motoring, another thing had occurred to Charlie. It was the reason that nobody had tried to contact him on his Qualcom, it was the reason he probably took his vacation in the first place.

No one will ever *need anything from you!!*

Outside, after he weakly heaved his baggage into the cab, he stared out at the horizon. A brief wind came gusting down some nameless mountain peak and hit him square in his scruffy face. It had been a nice day out, it was still around eighty degrees. But Charlie was shivering. Something other than the obvious was still not sitting well with him. His hands were cold and clammy, his legs felt like they weighed a couple hundred pounds each when he would move them, and the world seemed a little darker for some reason.

He looked over the ten. Its ugly, stupefied grin sat and smirked at Charlie, egging him on. Begging to be made an example of. He thought of Darla's face and grimaced before lighting up another Red. Rhiney was right about one thing, it suddenly clicked with Charlie that any infraction he made out on his playground, if she caught wind of it, she'd be tearing him a new one every day on the Qualcom. She would holler and shout and curse like all good bull dykes do. Something was certainly amiss with the entire situation. It was like when he went on vacation, everything was thrown out of whack.

He thought more about it as the Red dangled from his lips and he mocked his own enthusiasm as best he could doing his pre-trip inspection. The only reason he even performed the formality was because a bored local sheriff breezed by the frontage road a while back when he was schlepping his luggage out.

Ain't takin' no chances, no how, Charlie thought.

Then something even more bizarre occurred to him.

His load.

He had told the red, fire breathing injin on the IA border that he was hauling dry noodles. But had he ever bothered to check?

Charlie, whose mind was becoming fuzzier and deeper with each passing moment couldn't remember.

Your work is your work, the stale old voice of his playground called out to him almost mystically.

As his work boots thundered against the soft gravel of the parking lot, with each step his tired and under-circulated legs took, his heartbeat paced and paced. It was everything about the morning that bothered him, not just his general disregard for his duties. It was the strange pitch in the front desk clerk's voice, the coldness he felt all along his body, not just his face. It was the shadows. The loneliness.

As Charlie unhinged the latches on his trailer, another thought occurred to him. Maybe he really was starting to get sick. Maybe that thing on his face was beginning to infect the rest of him as the doctor had predicted. But he quickly pushed that notion aside, instead, he gathered what remained of his strength and opened the door to his trailer.

Inside blackness greeted him. It was as if he had uncovered a black hole somewhere deep in space. It spit out at him black, chilled wind. Nowhere in sight were any pallets or crates or boxes strapped down in their respective rows. No dry noodles, no other cargo, no nothing. There was only the blackness. It almost felt like something was watching Charlie out of the hole.

A couple of tiny red lights, floating in mid air.

The shadows overcastted much of Charlie's view and the sun seemed to disappear right before his eyes. Only grays and blacks and variations thereof lingered. Charlie felt the thing on his face frost over, icicles hung from his limbs, he felt like his hair had matted down into hard cubed clumps. And the darkness– besides it watching him, it almost seemed to call to him. Never had anything so lonely and so chilling possessed Charlie in the manner that it did. He felt like that child again, back in the gravel driveway of his boyhood shack in Sioux Falls. He felt like that boy pissing on the crumpled weeds, staring at the big silver moon, letting the warmth evacuate out of him. It was a feeling even Charlie couldn't shake off.

Here he was, in what felt like someone else's life, feeling the same thing all over again. The wind seemed like it had strengthened, the wayward hairs on Charlie's scalp danced around, the darkness grew grizzlier, the wind chill grew sharper.

Then, as if it had never been there at all– it disappeared in an instant. All that remained was a hollowed out trailer filled with nothing but dust mites and a peek of sunlight being allowed in by the crack of the trailer door. A few leftover red straps with broken hooks littered the floor from the last load, but that was it. And once again, Charlie was alone.

He burst up from his seat like a singular antelope would point its antlers to the sky when you would approach one on the highway. Cold, frosty residue that might have once resembled sweat protruded his face. His breathing had labored to the point where his heart seemed to flutter continuously. He lifted his leg and realized it had been on the clutch the whole time, he let it out, and the ten lurched forward with a groan. He stepped hard back on the clutch and the brakes, it shook to a jolting stop, hissing as air escaped. Something wasn't right. That was the only thing that was certain. Something wasn't right at all. But perhaps, the way Charlie figured anyway, it was time to set things right.

<u>25</u>

"Diesel Graveyards"

After a brief layover in Branson, Missouri, a hop, skip and a jump later, the two detectives were able to rest their feet in a taxi, carting them away from Sioux Falls International.

"Where to?" the cabbie asked in his dairy, cream-colored, Midwestern accent.

"Wait a minute, wait a minute," Aspen fumbled through the pages of his pocket notebook, until he sought the page he was looking for. "1609 Benson Road."

"You got it."

It was 9:30 in the morning on a particular gusty and gray day in Sioux Falls. The air was crisper than the usual Arizona jet stream the pair were used to. The atmosphere hinted at what lie in store for the upper Midwest in the coming months. They were silent, the farther they delved down the rabbit hole of this case, the more disconnected and dazed they became.

It didn't help matters that their family life was crumbling beneath their feet. In fact, right before they departed, Cynthia Aspen begged her husband to transfer to another department. She could no longer take the heavy baggage that came with being a detective's wife, at least not one involving this continually maddening investigation. He tried like hell to explain the importance of finding the answer and keeping the streak alive, but it fell on deaf ears. He had to fight pretty hard to even get a kiss as he walked out the door, on his way to the airport.

On the flight to South Dakota, the two detectives briefly discussed how the interview would be different than the one conducted at the hospital. Not only did they outline their specific questions for this Darla, they came up with a series of sub questions, depending on which path her answer would stray. They were locked, stocked and ready to go, desperately *needing* closure. Not because it was their job, not even because of their streak, but because of the voice that all natural born dicks are manufactured with at birth. It was relentlessly exhausting to have to answer to that voice, and the only way they knew how to make it stop was to find out the truth.

The classic yellow-checkered cab moaned its way out of the front lot. The detectives watched it go with a certain glazy disposition. They watched it turn east again on Benson Road, back towards the airport. Neither one of the detectives were looking forward to the interview the way they normally would. Customarily, they'd be chomping at the bit to talk to someone who knew the victim, but there had been far too many disappointments in the case, too many dead-ends. It had taken too much out of them. That, combined with the dreariness of the morning was enough to make them both ashamed of the fact that for the first time, they were treating it as a job.

The front entrance was merely a single, misaligned door outlined with a cheap wooden frame. A sign posted above it read, *Public Entrance.* Hesitantly, detective Aspen wandered up to find that it was locked. He glanced at his watch to double check the time. It was 9:53 in the morning. A cool wind swept across the flat point of Benson Road and blew his overcoat up, making it look like a cape. His eyes floated and noticed a Hawk a good hundred yards up, free floating in the wind. "There aren't any hours posted," his voice shuddered.

Tucker remained expressionless, he walked over to the window and cupped his hands over his face in an attempt to peer into the shadowy office. When that proved fruitless, he scanned the front lot. There was a beat up old Chrysler fixated in a corner spot, rusting away along a battered green wire fence. A brown 4x4 truck was a couple of spots away from it, a personalized South Dakota license plate read *Beast* hung from one corner of its gaping mouth.

"Damn, it's cold," Tucker sputtered, the stiff breeze picking back up.

"Let's go take a look around back," Aspen offered, taking the lead.

They followed another wire fence along side the office. The concrete under their feet stopped, and gravel took over. The stucco side of the building had occasional random roots and weeds peeking out of its aging cracks. Once they cleared the wall, an opening appeared in the fence and the yard presented itself.

There were a couple of guys down by the rows upon rows of trailers, dressed in flannel shirts, holding cups of steaming Joe and gunning sticks. A garden variety of different tractors rested on the other side, in varying stages of maintenance. A lime green Freightliner had its hood partially ripped off and the passenger door was hanging from its hinges. It appeared as if someone was in the middle of hooking up airlines from a trailer to a red Peterbilt, but the project was hastily abandoned. A more traditional diesel mechanic was busy gutting what was left under the hood of a beat up yellow Sterling.

The detectives managed to make their way around the building without being noticed by those in the yard. Its vast dirt and gravel landscape sparkled strikingly, even under the dull sky. The investigators came upon a rustic metal staircase leading up to what appeared to be the main office for drivers and yard monkeys. As they ascended the steps, the door at the top burst open and a huge mountain of a man in overalls and a larger than life beard with matching mutton chops came lumbering out. He was accompanied by a thick, robust woman who was dressed in olive cargo pants and an insulated flannel vest shouting loudly at him.

"And I tell this guy, 'your shipment will arrive in three days, dude.' 'I can't control the goddamn weather,'" the woman crows in a bawdy voice to the mountain man, who smirks and nods. "And still he's bitching at me. Finally I told him, 'Look here, no one can do nothing about no snowstorm, I ain't puttin' my drivers life in danger for someone I done business with for years, lettalone you.' And I hung up the phone on that sumabitch. That there was the last I heard from'em. And sure as shit, his load was delivered just three days later. Just like a told 'em." She cackled some more and they descended the stairs. "Shit. Tellin' me how to run my own business."

"That's tellin' 'em, Dar," the mountain man playfully hit her on the arm.

"Excuse me," Detective Aspen intervened, stopping the pair halfway in their tracks.

"Yeah, what do you want?" Darla asked defensively.

Already the two detectives saw they had their hands full. "We are from the Gila County Crime Division. I couldn't help overhearing your name was Darla. You are the proprietor of this business, then?"

"That's right. I'm Darla. What do you fellas want?"

"We would like to speak with you about Charlie Coldbrick. We need to ask you a few questions. It won't take long."

A gigantic, exaggerated and exasperated sigh escaped from Darla's diaphragm. "That bastard Coldbrick is gonna haunt me till the day I die, ain't he?" But she was no longer in a jesting mood. She and the mountain man who stood beside her, both of their demeanors changed somehow. The looks upon their faces became as drab as the morning and situation itself. They might have been mirrored by the shape the detectives were in. It would have been obvious to any third party observing– none of the individuals wanted to be involved with the situation they were currently in.

"You can wait in my office– in there," she lazily stuck a thumb out behind her. "I gotta go see bout somethin'. I'll be back in a moment."

"Thank you, ma'am," Tucker said patronizingly as he passed her.

The mountain man sheepishly trailed behind her, as if he were her loyal and uncorrupted servant.

"Lloyd! What's going on with the goddamn eight?" She yelled at one of the two loitering smokers, indicating the Peterbilt in its middle stages of repair.

He murmured something back in a calm voice that neither of the detectives could hear.

"Well get that mother out the way! I got Sanford coming in from Missoula in an hour and he ain't gonna be too pleased to see you jewin' his spot after three weeks on the road!" she screamed at the top of her lungs.

Before traipsing into the outer office of 1609 Benson Road, the two detectives marveled at Darla. They stood on the top stoop of the staircase and watched her interact with her staff. Even in their muddled moods and aching minds, they were able to note that Darla ran this yard like a drill sergeant on pep pills. She seemed to be a sturdy woman who took guff from no one, and would go toe to toe if need be. And at five foot three, no matter how tough she was, that was no simple feat.

They crept through the outer office at a snail's pace, it was filled with shabby looking map booklets, vacation request sheets, tax applications, and other employee relation forms. "That's a colorful woman," Aspen commented mildly to Tucker, obtaining a second wind as they approached the inner office, presumably Darla's office.

"Got a lot of fire," Tucker muttered back, unable to match the miniscule amount of enthusiasm his partner evoked.

Behind the door was Darla's Office all right. It was well maintained; files and folders were meticulously placed on what looked like newly installed shelving. Newer road atlases and carbon copies of legal contracts from shippers were placed in baskets with posted headings in bold letters. Headings like **SHIPPERS, TRACTORS, TRAILERS, TRIPS, TAXES, DRIVERS,** ect. Not only did this woman run a tight ship, but she was well organized too. Tucker secretly thought it reminded him of his own office. It was free of outside distractions and well oiled to serve the worksite's best interests. The only sign of anything leisurely was a water cooler placed against the inside wall, bubbling up as more purified H20 seeped through its filter.

The detectives were glad they had a moment to size up this Darla character before they went to work on her. That was after all, an integral part of their jobs, they had to be judges of character in addition to evidence, hearsay, and ultimately the truth. But this was different than preparing something for the DA. They both suspected that charges would not be filed in this particular case. This was the harder of the two kinds of cases that came their way. They were both still sure they would get to the bottom of it, but the pity of it was, once they were done, it would simply be filed away under accident. They would be able to fill in the cause of death on this Coldbrick fella's certificate of expiration. Judging by all the dead ends they had encountered, it wasn't likely that anyone would ever notice. They had nothing to show for it, which is why their enthusiasm waned with each passing day.

Large and unapologetic footsteps came thrashing towards the office, and in stepped Darla. "I tell ya guys, some days it just doesn't pay to get outta bed."

"Tell us about it," Aspen replied, glancing briefly at Tucker.

Darla zigzagged around the investigators with a look of extreme purpose on her face, like she was on a mission. Then, casual as can be, she plopped down into her rolling chair behind her desk. "You fellas can take a seat if you like," she outstretched her rubbery arm toward the two stiff chairs on the other side of her podium.

"I'm fine standing. We had one too many layovers this morning to be sitting again," Aspen chuckled at his own inane attempt to lighten the mood as he looked back to Tucker one last time.

They had decided on the plane that he should do the talking for this one. He was certainly the more personable of the two with his boyish and non-threatening demeanor. And as much as Tucker hated to admit it, Aspen had a better track record with witnesses in the past. Plus, he was from the Midwest, so he spoke Darla's language to some degree.

"We won't take up much of your time, Darla. We just have a few questions that are eating us up, and we think you may be the person to answer them. And I'm sure you have a few questions of your own, involving this incident."

"I don't know what more I can tell you fellas. And I already know what happened. I just as soon put this whole thing behind me, and Pioneer Trucking feels the same."

"So," Aspen started, feeling like he was back into old form, "you did get our messages? We've been trying like hell to get a hold of someone here for the past several days. I'm sure you've been busy, but a return phone call would have helped a great deal." He paused to take a breath, "But, nevertheless we are here now. So how long have you worked here, Darla?"

"First of all, I did call. And I've only been here a month in a half, don't you fellas share files or something? How many times do I gotta answer these questions?"

"Who else has interviewed you? Are you talking about Sioux Falls PD?" Aspen asked. He was becoming a tad perplexed at her assumptions.

Tucker stared out the window overlooking the bustling yard, but was surely listening intently. His ears worked like tiny antennas, and his huge hands gripped the high-powered tape recorder he'd brought along. The investigators had decided to change up their tools a few days previous since their last interview had gone so poorly. Gone were the chicken scratches on note pads, in was the highly sensitive microphone that recorded to magnetic reel to reel.

"Yeah, Sioux Falls PD, but you guys too. You fellas are from New Mexico, ain't you? How many agencies are involved with that old fart's death? What he do? Threaten the President or somethin'?"

Tucker turned around with a strange sort of smirk on his face, glaring at the situation from every angle. Aspen's heart sank below elevation in his chest, he actually stopped short because the wind felt like it had been knocked out of him. Something was desperately wrong, and with the urgency that seamlessly thrust itself on the detective's faces, Darla sensed it too.

"No. Nooo. We are not from New Mexico. I told you, we are from Gila County. That's Arizona. What does New Mexico have to do with it?"

"You mean you fellas ain't from– ah shit– what was the name they said? Colfax?" Darla leaned forward to confirm it on the giant calendar that sat on the top of her desk. She was paying special attention to a scribbling on September 18th. "Yeah, Colfax County, New Mexico? Because that's who I talked to."

"What? What did you say?" The feeling of losing all oxygen was coming back to Aspen at a frantic rate.

"Yeah, must'a been around two and a half, three weeks ago now. It was here –" she pointed at the calendar to illustrate the point, "September 18th."

Aspen took a few slow steps toward her desk as she rotated the calendar, staring at her all the way. Not wanting to believe any of it. He took his time looking down, but when he did, he read her scribbled note that exclaimed, *Colfax Cty. for Coldbrick the prick.*

As the thundering sound of his heart between his ears continued, he heard his own voice mutter, *"This is impossible."*

"I'm telling you, son. COL-FAX-COUN-TY-NEW-MEXICO." Darla spoke loudly, but slowly – as if she were speaking to a couple of adolescents that were having a rough time getting the picture. She was becoming agitated, but her face gave a hint of concern for what the detectives had been saying. Her bushy brow lowered and furrowed, her jello-y chin wavered like a flame in a windstorm.

"We are talking about the same Charlie Coldbrick?" Aspen managed to choke out.

"I hope to Lord and heaven there is only one of that asshole."

"Why do you say that, Darla?" Tucker asked with calmer nerves and lower blood pressure than his partner.

"Every one who ever knew 'em known that he was nothing but an S-O-B. I only actually met 'em once, but he was what you might call *an asshole*. Thought he was too big for his britches. Thought his shit don't stink. That last trip I sent him out on, he showed up late. And not a day had passed and I got a call from a DOT station on the IA border, tellin' me how he caused a big scene. Cussin' out the employees, stirrin' up trouble. His resume is full of that type-a shit. I heard stories from the other drivers, and other people from other companies. Ain't nobody want to work with him."

At that moment, even Tucker was taken back by the description of the deceased. Aspen's jaw was stuck near the floor and stayed there. It was quite a different account of the man they heard the first interviewee describe. The problem with both of Darla and Abby's testimonies was they both had only met him once.

The investigators didn't know what to believe, and both were far too stunned to think of anything to say. It was if the sky had opened up and it began raining fire. Everything was turned upside down. Nothing made any sense anymore. They said 'A' and everyone else said 'Z'. Worst of all, they knew their time with the witness was short…and impatient. Darla's threshold was hanging by a string, and they both knew it. And there was no way in hell they could have obtained an interstate summons to force her to talk. The case was all but dried up.

Finally, Detective Aspen broke from the trance he was in, desperate to get the information he could. "Can you tell us what the other agency told you, Darla? Because you are obviously more informed than we are." He shook his head sullenly, as if he just learned of a death of a close confidant.

The deep sigh she bestowed on them earlier had returned, "I dunno, he was in some hole-in-the-wall-motel on the New Mexico / Colorado border. Some flea-bag room off the highway…shit I can't remember what it was called. Anyway, he was in there a couple of days until the motel manager busted down the door and found him. I dunno what he died from, and they didn't tell me nothin' else. The only other thing I got after I talked to them was a message on my phone bout a week ago-" she stopped, seeming quite unsure about her statement. "Wait a minute– that was you." She lifted a finger towards Tucker, singling him out like a witness would a defendant at a trial. "I thought I recognized your voice, you don't look or sound nothin' like the other two fellers from Colfax County."

"This can't be happening." Aspen reiterated; he still sounded skeptical of Darla's entire testimony. He said it as if they were secret guests on *Candid Camera,* and someone was playing an unbelievable and mean spirited practical joke. "What about the tractor/trailer then? Did they say where that went?"

"They told me they would give me a call once they were done lookin' it over. I wasn't too concerned about that because I gave Coldbrick the ten. That beater was on its last leg anyhow. That's another thing, he was real pissy with me about that the day that I met him. Kept tellin' me how the fella that ran the place before me would always give 'em the five. And by now, you fellas know that I don't appreciate no one tellin' me how to run my business."

"Unbelievable," the words rushed from Aspen's lips.

"What is?" Darla asked as she rose from her seat, growing tired of the interview. "What do you fellas need from me? I can only tell this story a few more times before I look as crazy as you two do."

"Give us the number that Colfax County left with you," Aspen demanded, tired of the conversation himself. Worse yet, he was beginning to feel physically ill. Another moment in Darla's office would be enough for him to vomit that terrible airplane food he ingested earlier, all over her nice, neat floor. And he supposed as anyone might, that she wouldn't take too kindly to that.

After another one of her famous sighs screeched past her lips, she bent down to flip through her Rolodex, "A please might be nice. Ain't you fellas got any manners down there in Arizona?"

She produced the card and handed it over to Tucker since he was the closest. Aspen danced around the water cooler near the window, overlooking the yard, trying desperately without much success to keep his sickness at bay. "Are you two gonna tell me what your frettin' about?"

"We could Miss Darla, but you wouldn't believe us anyhow," Tucker leaned against her desk as he scribbled down the number for the contact in Colfax County on his trusty notepad. All the while he abandoned the reel-to-reel, still spinning on the windowsill.

"Sounds to me like you fellas came North for nothin'," she took her original card back from him.

"I'm afraid you might be right."

<u>26</u>

"The World Left Behind"

As the nappy, wayward golden straws of grass growing every which way started to bed down for the night, darkness also collapsed on Charlie. Not only did the goddamn glorious sun retreat back under the earth, but his trek through the lowly Cristo Mountains had cast more shadows than it ever would have in the daylight. Charlie kept the rig on the road, which happened to be a feat in itself. The windward pressure slammed against the tractor like it was a child's toy. Right in front of him, a couple of hundred yards down the road, a giant tumbling boulder crash landed and created a smoking crater that burnt red amber.

Then, when Charlie blinked, it was gone again. But not before he had stabbed his breaks twice and swerved so vigorously that the off tracking of the trailer nearly pulled the kingpin right from its jaws.

But Charlie hardly cared enough to stop and check. He didn't feel like sleeping ever again. He would do what he was asked to do, drop of his load in Tempe. After that – well – Charlie couldn't see that far. The entire landscape of his future was shrouded with the darkness that surrounded him. He wasn't quite sure that he even wanted a future. The easiest thing for him to do would have been nothing. It would be to let that goddamn piranha on his cheek eat him up until there was nothing left to eat.

But what about the world that is left behind? he brutally recited to himself. *What about my goddamn legacy?*

Charlie felt that it was his opportunity to leave his imprint on the world, if ever it had passed him up (and it probably did while he was out on some seven-seven binge) it was flirting its way back into his line of sight. The only question left for Charlie was

Will I take it?

But after that, he decided that would have to be enough for now.

Lotta goddamn miles between here and Tempe. Lotta time to think.

There were at least two decisions that Charlie was able to check off of his final "to-do" list. One, he would never again fall asleep in this world, and two, this was to be the last load he would ever drop.

That there has to be enough for now, he settled it by pounding his doughy fist on the steering wheel and pulling the string to sound off his horn, giving the local wildlife a little wakeup call of his own. If this too proved in time that Charlie was wrong– then– according to the man himself, it would be the last.

<u>27</u>

"Furious Angel"

Charlie drove. The sharp air whistled through the slit he left in his window, it sang to him. It sounded to Charlie like it did the first time, his playground sounded like it was whispering to him in caressing, yet abrasive tones. He let Las Vegas pass him in all its rickety, broken-down, former glory. A ramshackle village on the edge of the great Rockies, half full of illegal tacos and the other half inbred mountain folk who Charlie wouldn't piss on to save their lives from third degree burns. Or so he told himself.

Someone outta break into them White Sands missile bases and blast this hick haven to kingdom come, Charlie cited as he adjusted his side mirror. He barely gave the faded lights that sullenly diluted behind him another thought.

For the briefest of moments, he imagined he was driving a souped up, futuristic war machine. The kind he used to read about in his comics as a kid. He imagined he left a trail of red-hot fire in his wake. That he was turning the world behind him into lava. That he was a fallen angel that made the world suffer as he had.

He chuckled to himself when he had had enough. His mind was numb from thinking, but somehow he had felt it was sharper than ever before. He had actually convinced himself he was a great destroyer of the world. Everywhere he looked he saw red, and it had given him some extra sensory power that Charlie rarely felt.

<u>28</u>

"A Trial Run"

By the time he had reached the west end of Sante Fe, twenty miles from the heart of downtown. The sun began to rise again. And it too, was red. As red as the blood that had stained Charlie's cheek, as red as the fire that burned in his eyes. It ravaged the sky and made it scream in agony. Voices cried out from its surface, it harmoniously fused with the whispering of his playground. To add to the symphony, Charlie turned up the static of Sesame Street at full volume. Then he lit a Red to listen to the thin paper sizzle.

By early afternoon, Charlie had reached the outskirts of Albuquerque. He decided to ratify one of the earlier promises he had made himself, which was to stop long enough to buy a few more packs of Reds (*the last sticks I'll ever gun*, he thought briefly as he pried them out of the cashier's gangly fingers when he bought them) and also to give his snake a choke.

An inkling of fatigue crept down his spine, but he countered it by drowning out the stars as he cranked up Sesame Street. An old geezer whose voice he thought he recognized was telling a joke to the street about a time a guy woke up next to a gay, Hasidic Jew he mistook for his wife at a party the night before. Charlie didn't think the payoff was nearly as good as the build up to it. He switched it off when the man turned a cheek and started slinging bullshit about how more should be invested into the Jews.

Sounds like a tree huggin' pushpot, like he's actually takin' symp-athy, Charlie thought disgustedly to himself.

Many thoughts raced through Charlie's mind, both of the past and future. The short lived future it may be.

But there's still time, his stubborn mind insisted. *Still time for your legacy. Still time for the world to breathe your name through tremblin' lips.*

He was halfway to Socorro when it came to him in the form of a rusty old weigh station with no tractors in line. With his newly invigorated senses, Charlie could see a bored looking DOT bear just waiting for some action. He whizzed by him at the mandated seventy-five mile per hour speed limit, and the moment he did, the bear's face lit up like a pinball machine.

It was as if the world had slowed, and then lit up for Charlie. Some bright, beaming light opened up the sky above the mountains and shone through like a laser cutter, setting the majestic pines ablaze. The horizon shimmered through his windshield that was blemished with bug guts and bird shit, set to dancing by the waves of smoldering heat. By giving the Diesel bear some action, Charlie realized right then and there he had already set his legacy into motion.

"He's gonna call the pigs," he croaked through his jagged teeth to no one in particular. His heart picked up a beat, like when he saw that lizard oozing her way out of the shed up in Colorado. He repeated his statement, but this time through the lanky wires and etherfuzz of Sesame Street. "He's gonna call the fuckin' pigs!"

Some trucker with the handle Marmalade Maryman answered him hoarsely after a couple of minutes, "Boy, you better turn right round back there on your knees and hope that bear don't mind you're a dude!"

Annoyed, because the statement– no– the revelation was meant to be rhetorical, Charlie switched the CB off. "Fuck em'," he whispered calmer, realizing at the same time that he had passed many a weigh stations within the last few weeks. He had always followed the rules loosely, but he tried to be smart about it and cover up his muddy tracks.

He would make up his comic as he went along. He would produce fake DOT inspection stickers to make himself look semi (no pun intended) legit. But on this trip to TEMPE, all that had flown out the window in a lustrous wind so brutal that it even cold-cocked Charlie a bit.

But Marmalade Maryman was wrong, it was too damn late. Even if he wanted to turn around and play by the rules, Charlie was double fucked. He was about to cross into the Jemez range where there wouldn't be another exit for several miles. And if that bear called the sheriff, one of the fleet pigs would nab him by then.

Charlie kept on driving, glancing in his mirrors irreverently, almost excitedly, even slowing down a bit, tempting fate all the more. He caressed the buck knife in the breast pocket of his denim jacket, quickly and carefully going over the schematics of his newly evolved idea. He decided the best way to leave a legacy would be to exact the revenge on the very species that caused him so much grief over the years– at least one of them anyway. It was either that or try and figure out some way to take out the sun. But since the latter was by Charlie's, and all of mankind's standards, impossible, it would have to be the former. Take out a few DOT pigs. Lop of their black, withered balls and tits.

Any goddamn minute those cherries will be lighting up the valley ahead of me. Any goddamn minute now.

Charlie licked his chops, eagerly awaiting the sight of them when the road careened to show the miles ahead. His foot flirted and goosed all the pedals, shaking from the excitement.

Even in Charlie's state of mind, he knew what he planned to do was neither fruitful, nor legendary. He knew that. He knew that even though it would make the news that some psychotic fucker carved up a half dozen New Mexico state troopers (because he reckoned he would get that many) that those types of scenes were a dime a dozen. He knew that his plan was neither new, nor bold. He knew that people have those shameful thoughts every day whether they are going to cross the thin line and execute the plan or not.

But Charlie settled on the idea that if, even for a day (or at least a couple of passing moments) the world knew his name, if they *needed* to be reminded of the tale of crazy old Charlie Coldbrick, that there would be good enough. And it was **that** that made his blood shiver in ecstasy and his eyes dart around like a kid's would in the world's greatest candy store.

That excitement never waned, because he knew his moment was coming. He had sensed it when he passed the I-40 junction an hour or so back. The newfound vigor didn't even have the heart to simmer as he made his way past Lemitar and Escondida. Sure, Charlie began to wonder, but his speculation was all too brief, like when he silently inquired as to why Darla the dyke never called him when he didn't show up for his destination.

It looked to Charlie that he might never make it to TEMPE after all. His excitement never faded enough to cause him to think lucidly, because he knew there were countless chances left before he would ever reach that down and dirty desert sub section of Phoenix.

Lotta miles left, lotta chicken coops left to be fled. Lotta hungry diesel bears left out there. Whoever the pig is, they ain't gonna know you bite back til it's too goddamn late.

His mind repeatedly reiterated it over and over. That was what kept Charlie going as he crawled through Socorro like the mountain rattlesnake. He caught the tiniest, briefest of glimpses of the Rio Grande until I-25 swung hastily west again.

<u>29</u>

"Ma Bell Screaming into the Night"

The detectives aimlessly spun theories and hypothesis that rivaled only the JFK assassination in the hours following the interview with Darla.

That Charlie guy must have had an identical twin. No, he was an alien that was able to morph into any object he touched, which would explain the different testimonies from the two witnesses regarding his personal character. No, someone set this up, they killed Charlie in New Mexico and drug his sorry carcass all the way to Arizona in a half baked plot to overthrow the government. Maybe this was a new form of psychological terrorism. We were probably right the first time, something has been spiked into the water supply of the greater Sioux Falls area.

As they sat in their hotel, a *Comfort Inn* just off I-90, each hypothetical dart they threw was more outlandish than the next. It was like trying to find a particular intersection in a town with no street signs. This case was lost in the worst way possible. They had never even come close to this loose a grip on a conclusion. The wayward feeling each of them had, but failed to express to one another as they rocketed into town on a charter flight from Branson felt even more intense.

It seemed their much-coveted streak was all but over.

Later that night, after conversation had dried up, Aspen began to complain of an upset stomach and called it a night. Besides their paranoid conspiracy conversation earlier, he had remained quiet most of the day.

Tucker, on the other hand, couldn't sleep. He lay awake while his eyes spun around the room. They stared fixatedly at the ceiling, they looked on piercingly past the inane late night television infomercials, and every so often they would come to rest on his partner who turned in early. Tucker knew full well what was coming next. Most likely his associate deep in his slumber did too.

So why was his mind whirring and spinning the way it was? The case had obviously driven way past ordinary – that much was for sure. But something still bothered him about it as he rested his body among the rusty springs of an otherwise comfortable double bed.

It was mostly likely due to the fact that they had yet to contact the guy, Bradford, in Colfax County, New Mexico. When they arrived at their hotel following a wayward, silent breakfast at a local *Country Kitchen*, they argued over who would make the call to the contact Darla had given them. They were desperately seeking closure to the case, but at the same time, both were terrified of the answer that awaited them. Maybe that was why they had formulated all the maniac suppositions. They *needed* that escape before the brutish realties of the world came flooding back in. It certainly wasn't very professional of them. It certainly wasn't the actions a distinguished pair of veteran investigators such as themselves were known for making. For that, Tucker felt the most ashamed.

What would the chief say?

Funny thing, as much as the case was crumbling beneath their feet, so was their faith in their occupation. Tucker loved what he did, always had. He knew the moment he was sworn in that it was what he was destined to do. To find the answers that no one else could. And now, because of one strange case whose answer was probably just around the corner, he was going to give that up?

As he stood up, he noticed his shadow repeating his movements from the glare of the television on the wall. For the briefest of moments, he thought about waking his partner, but then decided against it. He calmly made a move toward his overcoat that he draped over the upholstered chair in the corner, and quietly slipped out of the room. He wanted to take a walk, to clear his head. He thought about his family, his sick daughter who was finally on the mend. He thought about what might lie ahead, and ever so briefly– what might lie above.

What else would Tucker do if he weren't an investigator? It's the only thing he's ever known, and he was good at it.

What else *could* he do?

He walked on as he thought about these things and many more. There was no way he could have known how much time had passed. Tucker was trapped in one of those restless, dreamlike states that renders time rhetoric. The kind of dazed, psychotropic journey that someone of his sound mind and proper manner would never have imagined taking.

A slow rain began to tumble down from the sky as he approached the intersection of Potsdam and Lewey. A lonely boarded-up service station stood on one corner, and wet dew stained weeds and brown open grasslands with chain linked fences off in the distance stood on the other three. The raindrops hit the warm asphalt of the road and created tiny little explosions of mist and vapor. The streetlamp that highlighted the intersection blinked on and off as if someone was flipping the switch continuously.

A pole stuck out of the ground about six feet high under the pulsating, illuminated area. Attached to it was an ancient mechanism Tucker had figured died out long ago, but its blue, white and orange colors spoke loud and clear. The permanently stained Plexiglas, the huge bible hanging from its metal binding, the metal protected cord that connected the handset to the receiver and the exclamation near the top that proclaimed the loudest of all, **BELL**.

A phone booth stood at this obscure corner of the world, with a jittery spotlight hanging over it. Tucker didn't believe in signs, nor did he believe he was any less skeptical of his job than he ever was. "Everyone has doubts," he quietly told himself as he pulled up the collar of his overcoat and hiked over to the booth for shelter from his newly damp surroundings.

Before he knew it, he was pulling a scrap of paper out of his pocket, shoving all the quarters he had at his disposal into the apparatus and dialing a number in the 575 area code. Some fellow named Bradford King in New Mexico.

What are you doing? It's nearly 11:30 mountain time. Do you honestly believe this Bradford guy is at his desk? In his office? He's at home sleeping under the same roof of his wife and 2.3 kids.

But the line was already ringing, the ring sounded strange, like it was tone deaf. He figured at first that if for some miraculous reason this ancient booth still worked, that the line would be garbled, or at least there would be interference from the rain. But the sounds came through crystal clear.

Tucker began to plan on what he would say in the message he would leave for Mr. King, but before he decided upon anything, the line on the other end picked up.

It was silence, or at least the phone had stopped ringing. But a piercing, ominous nothing greeted Detective Tucker. No sign of breathing or life of any kind.

It was simply nothing.

Tucker licked his lips, assuming he had missed the beep for the machine and was about to begin speaking. A tired, but high-pitched squeaky voice finally came through on the other end, "Colfax County, this is Bradford."

The voice sounded so animated, so surreal, so unauthentic that Tucker remained speechless in disbelief. But after another moment, he regained his composure to croak, "Hello?"

"Hello?" the voice answered back harmoniously, but a bit more realistic.

"Hi –" Tucker stammered, surprised at himself because he was never stumped so easily. "Hi, I'm sorry – I didn't think anyone would be there, I was going to leave a message."

"How can I help you?"

"My name is Desmond Tucker, I'm an investigator for Gila County, Arizona. I'm calling from Sioux Falls, South Dakota and am currently investigating the death of a Charlie –"

A higher pitched screaming noise so horrible and so blood curdling interrupted the detective mid sentence. Instant gooseflesh began to pop out onto his skin like the pockmarks of a pimply teenager who had developed into an awkward man. His stomach did a tilt-a-whirl and his body temperature felt as if it had plummeted twenty degrees.

Tucker wasn't sure if it was the same voice that answered the phone screaming, or if it was someone else that was sounding off. All he knew was that he had never been that startled since he was probably eight years old. The scream paused and then started up again, he also heard some fumbling of items on a desktop in the background. He held the phone away from his ear in an earnest agony. His heart skipped a beat or two. Then the screaming stopped, just as soon as it had started.

"Sorry about that," the voice on the other end seemed to change pitch with every sentence. "I was digging through my locker earlier and found this tape. I wanted to hear what was on it. We pulled that one from an investigation about five or six years ago. Cold file. That was the little artifact we found at one of the scenes. I hate screamers when you're trying to interview. You ever get those? The kind where you have to throw 'em into a cell when you think your head is gonna fly off your neck." The supposed Bradford King's voice continued to change, low then high. It sounded far away and then like he was shouting right into the phone. None of it made any sense to Tucker. He took an awkward silent breath and began to wonder if he had dialed the right number.

Hadn't he answered 'Colfax County'?

"Why are you telling me this?" Tucker's voice was not quite back to it's full gravely state, but close enough.

"Because, that is what this fucking case makes me want to do! Charlie's case. It makes me want to scream until my larynx rots! It makes me want to shout up to whatever sick bastard inhabits the sky until my eye balls fall out of my head! This is torture. That's why I'm not doing it anymore." Bradford took a long pause. Tucker thought he had set the phone down, but then he came back, erupting the silence by clearing a frog from his throat. "Well now –" his real voice seemed to have floated back to him. The volume was no longer erratic, and the pitch had managed to sustain itself. "Damn, I've been waiting for that all night. So then – you're up awfully late. Where did you say you were calling from again?"

"I'm calling from Sioux Falls, South Dakota. The woman who gave me your number tells me you were out this way a few weeks ago."

"Yeah, my partner and I were investigating a death. It was so strange they would send us out all that way. There was never any sign of foul play. It should have been open and shut. We told them, we told all of them. Then the coroner's report came back and we said, 'See? Told ya so, now didn't we?'"

"What was it?" Tucker asked, able to ignore the obvious nonsense that made up his case and apparently Bradford's in New Mexico. Able to put forth his suspension of disbelief in order to obtain the coveted truth.

He was still sure enough of himself and his abilities to be able to wade through the drivel and uncover what had really happened to this guy Charlie. Maybe no one from his life was even remotely curious, especially that Darla. But that is what a detective does; they either represent, or in this case, replace the concerned party. The welfare of mankind was Tucker's business, that much he knew. And the world would not rest until he figured out exactly what had happened. The case was a tough one for certain. But it would also be another exemplary gold star on his resume. Plus, he figured he might be able to take he and his partner's streak to the next level.

It's not dead yet, not just yet it's not.

"The man died of complications due to melanoma. Had we found out before we went to Sioux Falls, we might have been able to ask this Darla firecracker if she knew her employee was sick. Or at the very least, poke around his medical records a bit. But obviously– that's no longer possible."

"Why isn't it possible?"

"Because we were thrown off the case. I don't know who has it now. Maybe no one. Ever since the evidence fiasco, I don't know anything about anything anymore. And you know what? I don't care either. This is the most – the most –"

Tucker waited patiently for the rest, but it never came. Instead, the maniac on the other end of the line began to sob quietly. Much in the same way Abby did back at the hospital. This was more his partner's forte, which is why he still needed him. They might not always have had the best relationship, but Tucker realized how they complimented one another. Which is why the chief always insisted on keeping them together. That, and their streak surely spoke for itself.

Tucker was much tougher and more systematic than his partner, he was able to crack the hardest of the witnesses. Hard-nosed interrogation was his specialty. Dealing with the other end of the spectrum, the more human end, was Aspen's. So when Bradford King started to cry through the landlines all the way down from Colfax County, New Mexico, he was once again at a loss of what to do. It's not that he was inhumane; it's not that he didn't feel for the man. He must have screwed up quite badly to be at this point. He just didn't know how to handle it. So instead, he continued on with his line of questioning, sure that the answer would come.

"But was it like Darla said? Did he die in that motel room?"

"Yeah, but forget it. It's a dead end. I talked to the night manager ad nauseum, he remembered finding him, but they never found a record for when he checked in. The guy disappeared soon after that. Just like the foreman in the evidence garage. Just like I'm about to do. If you were smart, you would too."

"I don't think I can do that, you see –"

We have this streak, Tucker thought about telling him, but then realized it would make no difference.

"Sometimes the truth just doesn't want to be found. Sometimes it's better if we don't find it out."

"You don't sound like an investigator at all."

"I used to be one."

"Well, what happened at the evidence garage?" Tucker struggled momentarily to find a way to keep him talking.

"We had the truck. A big nasty old red thing. It looked like Charlie when we found it. Deader than Elvis. Then, it just disappeared."

There were those words again. Detective Tucker couldn't believe his ears. "Things don't just disappear."

"Then it was stolen out of the warehouse. I don't know. Like I said, I don't care any longer. I'm going to disappear myself. Something we don't understand touched this Charlie guy. I don't think I want to know what it is either. That's why I was listening to the tape. I want the screams to stop. You understand that, don't you Mr. Tucker?"

"Right now, I don't know the meaning of understanding," he whispered softly.

"I think I know what you mean." His voice pitched once again.

Tucker thought he heard something else, but then the line went dead. That automated voice came on, informing him that if he wanted the call to continue, he would have to deposit an additional fifty cents. Tucker declined.

Instead, he watched the rain fall in heavier bands against the pavement. Perhaps he was waiting for something to happen. Waiting for something to disappear.

<u>30</u>

"The Chill of Discombobulation"

None of it panned out for Charlie, of course. The disinterested minutes gave way to indifferent hours and no pig showed its snout. Not one that Charlie felt was *needed* to implement his artful, master plan.

He roared past the Southern Playas of New Mexico in the monster ten, he briefly glanced over the dried up ancient lakes; desert beaches save for an inch or less of water. They looked how he felt, on the verge of spewing death from every orifice. But Charlie could always feel the chill of death in the air around autumn time, no matter how close to the earth's core he tried to get. He thought it one of the most cloakable seasons, especially down in the Southern latitudes. Autumn always slips quietly across the desert, the chilly nights eradicate the greenery brought on by the stint of summer rain. The whole process turns the terrain a dusty olive to a bleached straw, until finally a weathered brown.

The sun eventually began to set again when a brand new, spotless sign presented itself beside the road, *Truth or Consequences, New Mexico*, it read. Charlie had glanced briefly at the roughed and ripped foam leaking from the ceiling of the ten, like he was pondering something very hard.

Which are you going to choose? his playground whispered to him when a north desert wind swooped up and swallowed the road.

"I chose consequences," Charlie told it calmly as he quickly ripped the truck up into eighth and thrusted the frightful engine to increase speed. All he had to get through was the Caballo range which was a weak set of hills that lie at the foot of his bigger, more intimidating brothers. Charlie suddenly remembered that he had to cut over to I-10 through the Cookes Range and avoid Las Cruces altogether. Plus, he hated to get too close to the border. There were too many tacos for his taste. And Charlie didn't want to waste any sizeable measurement of his energy on the likes of them.

As the sun retreated down, further and further, Charlie did something that even surprised himself and waved goodbye to it like a little kid. Soon after, the bright moon, waning from full a few days previous, illuminated in front of a crystal clear sky. As Charlie glanced at it, he felt a strange reverberation somewhere in his chest. He had suddenly wished he could have helped that woman who his Mom was so mean to all those years ago. She looked so distraught, standing in the Coldbrick's dirty, gravel driveway under a similar moon.

"NO!" he screamed at himself. "Don't get pink on me now!" he shouted to no one. He covered his mouth, but his mind still screamed: *That was so goddamn long ago, that it might as well have been someone else's life! 10-4, GOOD BUDDY?!*

Just when he thought he would abort his plan completely and give into the torturous world he had currently found himself in, a savior appeared in his bottom most side mirror. Its red and blue lights flashed dimly patriotic, an angel of liberty.

His ultimate sanctorum slowed along with him as he serenely put pressure on the break pedal, goosing the clutch along with it when he was down to third. He looked around at the dim landscape and sighed a heavenly breath.

If I were crem-ated, I'd probably wanna be scattered here. But Charlie decided never to make those kinds of preparations for his own mortality.

Hal once even suggested it, years ago, but Charlie laughed it off at the time. "Who in the hell am I going to get to scatter em'?" Charlie roared at Hal in his office when he arrived back from a three week trip out east. Hal just laughed that squeaky, dusty sounding laugh of his, but never answered him. Charlie, at the time, took it as Hal agreeing with him.

Who would Charlie get?

After all, *no one ever* needed *anything from him.*

<u>31</u>

"Living Proof"

It had been three days since the detectives returned from Sioux Falls, not much had changed during that time. Tucker did eventually update his partner on the strange circumstances involving his phone call to Colfax County. When he told him, Aspen had simply nodded, not really begging to hear the fragmented details that Tucker was able to piece together.

He tried to reach him once more, just to verify that it was indeed Bradford King he spoke to. He tried right before they were to check out from the *Comfort Inn*. The man's voicemail message came on, and the voice on the recording seemed to confirm what Tucker needed to know.

Aspen had remained silent the times he saw him at the office. Mostly, he would just hide out. It seemed to Tucker, in addition to everyone else that his spirit seemed to have shattered somewhere along the way on the Sioux Falls trip. He would rub his neck constantly, which may have suggested he was riding the couch. Tucker figured it meant he was still fighting with Cynthia over the case he seemed to have little or no interest in any longer.

Tucker was good at hiding his frustration over his partner's unenthusiastic attitude. It's almost as if Aspen were waiting for something to happen as well.

Tucker even looked the file over with another veteran in the Department, a guy named Pierce Kringle. He spent half an afternoon presenting the ridiculous and unbelievable details the pair had stumbled across thus far. Explaining how they had exhaustively searched all the normal avenues with little to no success. Pierce, five months away from retirement, told him that's one headache there is no elixir for. When Tucker pressed him, he suggested talking to the medical examiner. "There's no better witness to a death than the deceased themselves," Pierce spoke to Tucker as if he were speaking to a congregation. He used a politician's hand gestures and college professor's voice, "Just because they're dead, doesn't mean they can't tell you anything."

Truth be told, Tucker had lost his nerve. Maybe not as much as his partner had, but ever since he spoke to Bradford King in New Mexico, something in him had also changed. He was nervous about situations he had never been nervous about before. Something in that phone call had spooked him in a way. He didn't know if it was the abrupt screaming in the background, or if it was something particular that Mr. King had said.

Perhaps, it was the fact that he believed every thing that King had told him. If everything about that was true, then how the hell would he be able to go and talk to the Gila County medical examiner? What would he be talking to him about? The body of one Charlie Coldbrick that he saw with his own eyes that late September day in the middle of the desert. But how can the man's body be in Colfax County and Gila County at the same time?

There is also the rig. Tucker wished he had asked King when exactly the rig disappeared.

Someone could have stolen it and Charlie's body and brought it down here to Arizona. But why? What would that accomplish? What would it prove?

But that's not true, Mr. King alluded to an autopsy, which means they had to have the body.

Like a bottlerocket ready to launch out of the earth, Tucker sprung up and ran down the hall to the County clerk's desk. "Cheryl? Would you please find me the number to the medical examiner's office in Colfax County, New Mexico?"

The young twenty something that was on her first real job out of college sighed, and struck a pose that suggested she was beyond bored of the office life already. "Sure thing Mr. Tucker."

"Thanks."

After a few minutes spent pacing around the department, talking to random colleagues, Tucker returned to his office to find the number waiting for him on his desk. He thought about informing Aspen of his decision, but when he walked by his office, he saw that he was on a heated, personal call and thought it best to leave him be. Convinced that this Bradford was feeding him a line, Tucker carefully dialed the number and once again listened to the sound of telecommunications at its finest ring on the other end.

"Colfax Coroner's office, this is Stewart," a happy-go-lucky voice answered.

"Hiya Stew," Tucker thought at the last minute he would attempt the softer, more gentle approach his partner might have had he not been out of commission. "I'm calling from the Gila County Criminal and Civic division and wanted to inquire about a possible cadaver you might have had in your care, maybe a month or so ago."

"All right, just a moment, sir."

Tucker remained patient as he listened to the sound of the operator checking files on the computer. He was thankful he hadn't put him on hold, he had heard enough *musak* in the last two weeks from sitting on hold to last a life time. Briefly, Tucker's mind wandered back to what Bradford had said

It just disappeared

and

Something touched this Charlie guy

He had been racking his brain ever since about what he had meant by that. However, Stewart softly conversing with someone in his office broke his stream of consciousness. The only word Tucker was able to make out was *Arizona.*

A new voice came on the line, an obvious superior to Stewart. "Hello, my name is Doug, may I ask whom is calling?"

"My name is Desmond Tucker. I'm an investigator with Gila County. I need to check and see if you had a cadaver there recently. The name of the deceased was..." Tucker began to shuffle random papers around his desk, he wasn't sure why. He really didn't need a façade to obtain this information. Interdepartmental relations were usually pretty civil, especially when it came to harmless records like the kind Tucker was seeking. "...the name was Charlie Coldbrick."

"All right, just a moment."

This time Doug did put Tucker on hold, but it sounded like the answer was coming. So waiting through the electric string version of "Time has Come Today" seemed like much less of a chore.

This time it was Stewart that returned rather quickly with a sense of urgency in his voice. "Okay Mr. Tucker, we did have one by that name, and you were right, it was a little less than a month ago. We received it on September 13th. White male, 54 years old. According to the autopsy, died of complications due to melanoma."

Tucker drew in a sharp gasp, he was really preparing for the opposite. He was hoping that what Bradford had said was a load of bullshit. He calmed himself by taking a sip out of his Styrofoam cup, tepid water from the cooler down the hall and asked, "Are you folks still in possession of the body, then?"

"Oh no," Stewart was quick to answer again, as if something was plaguing him. As if some unfinished business was still lingering in his mind and he was afraid he would soon forget. "When no one claims the cadaver they usually end up one of two places, the University in Santa Fe, or another morgue. We just don't have the capacity here. I don't see in the file where this one ended up, but I suppose we could do some more digging."

"No," Tucker said, "Don't worry about it, that's enough to go on. Thank you for your help, Stewart."

<u>32</u>

"The End of a Legacy"

He slowed to a stop and cut the engine. Meanwhile, he realized his savor was in the form of an evil kinevil. The worst kind. The ones that hide out under over passes and billboards and the world's biggest whatever... They hide and they stalk and they prey. Charlie had been nabbed by them a few times before. *Once in Grand Island, Nebraska* he faintly remembered.

The pig had remained on its motorcycle for several minutes. Sweat oozed out of Charlie's forehead, running cruelly down his face and stinging the piranha on his cheek. He didn't wince or grab at it though. By that time, he had learned his best to ignore it or pretend it wasn't there. His heart was also a couple of miles over the limit and he suddenly remembered to check his jean jacket pocket. His trusty buck was still there, gleaming confidently in the pale moonlight.

Finally, the pig had planted its hooves out onto the asphalt, gracious enough to come down with the rest of the world. Charlie gasped sharply and flung open his door. "Showtime," he muttered to himself as he slammed it behind him and came down hard on his feet.

When he looked away for a moment, the pig had removed its helmet, revealing smooth yellow hair tied back in a ponytail. The helmet also gleamed as it rested on the hip of a young woman fresh outta pig preparation school. *Even better,* his playground breathed a final word into his ear.

"Evenin'," she smiled as she strode up to Charlie, stopping about two or three feet in front of him. One hand rested on her helmet and the other on her hip, close enough to her service revolver.

"Hi," Charlie croaked, tired as he was, he actually smiled back.

"License, registration and papers please," she continued to smile. She didn't look at him like a normal pig would. In fact, when Charlie met her gaze, he realized that as much as he hated her kind, she was one of the prettier ones he'd scene. She must have noticed the black bubble infested in his smile by now, but she kept on smiling anyway. She didn't scoff or sneer at him the way any other pig might. It almost seemed to Charlie like she was looking through him somehow. As if he wasn't standing on the road in front of her. The fact that her beauty couldn't even be tainted by the buck, ugly uniform she was draped in somehow startled him. It somehow made her more real. She smiled at him like the world was a camera lens and the entire population was looking through the eyepiece.

Charlie thought all those things, but then shook his head as she studied his papers.

"Been on the road a long time, I see," she beamed at him.

"Yeah," Charlie sighed, the tips of his fingers still deciding whether to go into his pocket. Because once he made that move, it wouldn't be long before the smile was flushed from her face and the conditioned pig defense mechanisms would creep in. "I ain't had much work lately and I'm tryin' to pro-lawn-g it as much as I can til somethin' else lines up."

For the first time, her smile half disappeared. She looked at him respectfully, if not a little doubtfully. It was as if she was trying to decide if she believed him or not. "Wouldn't your boss be mad at that? Not to mention who's expecting...what are you hauling exactly?" The smile returned almost as quickly as it left.

"Oh uh...dry noodles. Um, I'm droppin' em' off at a food wholesaler in... in..." Charlie stopped suddenly, a bright loud siren was going off in his head. He felt dizzy, but also a bit like that child back in the driveway of his shack. This time his playground's voice was haunted by that of his mother's.

No one will ever need anything from you!!! Just do it, you limpdick! Stab that bitch right through her black heart! You know what she represents! You're useless! Just like your limp dick father! No one will ever need anything from you!

"...TEMPE," Charlie finished, coughing slightly.

She looked him over for a long time; the smile faded some more, but it was still prominent enough. He hated her looking at him like that, because it seemed like it had gone on forever. Meanwhile, his playground was still cursing his name.

Your legacy! Your GODDAMN LEGACY, CHARLIE! COME ON, DIVE INTO THAT BED YOU MADE! YOU'RE GETTING TOO GODDAMN SLEEPY NOW!

Several times, his arm jumped at his side. He tried his best to control it, but it was much too antsy. It was like trying to guess when exactly Jack was going to pop out of his box. Any moment she was going to get suspicious and ask him what's wrong. Her face that was perfectly smooth and seasoned with dimples would change into the carnivorous succubus that she probably really was. Her eyes would be red fire, nervously grabbing at her pistol and her radio as Charlie would move in for the kill. But of course, by then, it would be too late. The end of his legacy would come first, and all the noble actions he planned on taking beforehand would be lost in the desert wind, being blown away like a tumbleweed.

Charlie sighed again, accidentally, uncontrollably, but worst of all loudly. She glanced up a bit more trepadiscious, yet still her smiled remained. The sigh was a manifestation of his internal struggle, but she must have taken it a different way. Her eyes veered toward a bittersweet sympathy that Charlie had rarely experienced. "You know," she started as she handed him back his license and registration, but keeping his papers firm in hand. "You don't seem like you're in the right frame of mind to be driving right now. Now, I'm not going to check your logbook, but I think you need a nap. My shift ends in a half hour and I gotta get back," and to the world's surprise, she actually winked at him.

"I'm just going to check on your papers, and you can be on your way...to a rest stop that is. I want you to get some sleep before you head off to Tempe." Besides her last sentence, she didn't even seem like a cop to Charlie, she seemed like a kind stranger that was showing genuine concern for her fellow man. It confused and angered him something awful inside. He wouldn't believe that a pig would be this nice. Part of him screamed that it was a savvy devil that was trying to trick him by using wiles other than the obvious ones.

"Okay," even his voice sounded confused, smaller, not as confident as he was when he exited the cab ready for the ultimate rumble.

She took no notice. And it seemed to Charlie that it was either because she was still in the deepest part of her game, or she was telling the truth and was almost ready to get off work. Either way, all of his anger was aimed directly inward. He felt his furious breath burn up his insides, turning them blacker than ten thousand lifetimes of sucking Reds.

"Good," her smile returned full bore. "Go ahead and get back in your cab, Charlie. It'll be a few minutes while I verify these."

Then, she performed another unbelievable gesture, something that even Charlie knew, the number one trick of the piglet trade. She trusted him enough to turn her back on him and mosey back toward her bike. Charlie's mouth hung open agape, the whispers his playground shouted were knocking the wind straight out of him. As he watched her yellow trusses bounce rhythmically as she walked at a steady pace, the voice screamed in satanic tones,

She thinks she's got you pegged. You need stop being such a fucking waste of life and waste a life! 10-4?!

Do it now!

He patted his jean pocket awkwardly, if his ears hadn't been drowning in white noise again, he would have been alarmed at how eerily quiet his gestures were.

She didn't turn around. Instead, she walked steadily back to her bike as if she were the only soul alive in the valley. A bird crowed somewhere off in the distance – a vulture perhaps. It slowly clicked for Charlie that it was now or never.

He pictured her bloody remains, strewn out all over the highway, looking like a bag of rustic autumn leaves. He pictured lighting bolts charging down and striking him, empowering him all the more. Or maybe just enough to give him the energy to waste a couple of the inevitable backups that would show their snouts soon after.

He felt like dropping to the sandy ground and breaking down into tears. The shame poured into his head with the pressure of a fire hose. He wished right then and there that he would have gone after her and did it slowly enough to where she'd be forced to defend herself by offing him. Suddenly, the noble parts of his plan just didn't seem important to Charlie any longer.

Then do it! There's still enough goddamn time! Pull out your buck and charge her! Charge and wail at the top of your lungs like those wild, savage injuns! Scream bloody murder at her until she quiets your world for good!

But Charlie's body wouldn't listen. Instead, he slinked back into his tractor, five or so feet off the ground, but feeling the lowest he had ever felt. Obviously, Charlie had done some awful things in his existence, but all of those rolled up into one didn't compare to how he felt at the moment.

As he sat in his sweaty seat, he felt soiled and chilly. The fact that he let himself down was enough to drive mad torment through his head for the next ten years.

She reappeared, hoisting herself up to his window. "Here's your papers, Charlie," her smile shining through the toffee colored night. "Don't worry, I'm sure you'll get back on track tomorrow. Right after you have that nap."

She gave him a little wave as she revved and aimed her cycle down the valley at a frantic speed. Charlie watched her go in seething, somehow jealous rage. He couldn't understand how a person of her ilk could be so happy. He thought briefly about how someone is probably expecting her, a significant other perhaps. That would have explained why she was so anxious for her shift to be over.

Charlie nodded to confirm it, sucking in deep breathes through his throat, and it almost seemed, the hole on the tip of his cheek.

She gots somewhere to be all right. Right now someone young, dumb and full of come is waitin' for her back at the sub station, he thought. They are probably so fresh, that he keeps checkin' the clock in his pickup, then he keeps peepin' at the highway, nervous like, waitin' for her. His mind is probably doin' a tornado, he's probably thinkin' about how to get with her tonight. He's thinkin' about what he'll say, how he'll say it, maybe he's even thinkin' bout what she'll say too.

Right now, someone needs *her in the worst way possible.*

Maybe that's how come the jealous rage for Charlie.

In a split second, his finger caressed the push button ignition, all by itself. His body was fixing to take control of the diesel dog and run her right down.

Might be a few minutes till I'm able to catch her, but after that, she'd be nothin' but a yellow grease-spot in the granny lane.

He pulled his hand away as if it were next to a flame, it felt hotter than the inside of his head. Charlie buried his aching skull in his hands and listened to the high wind howl outside his cab.

He took himself out of the semi for a moment– maybe more than a moment. He was a bird, watching this yellow haired evil knievel burrow down the highway at breakneck speed. He watched as she let the red rock eat the dust of her motorbike, as she barreled toward the one that *needed* her most, whoever it may be.

When the wind changed directions, a light pebble flew into his surrogate eyes, banishing him back to the inside of the cab. He looked around wearily at the cooling empty valley and let himself alone. For the briefest of moments, that stagnant hospital aroma crept back into his nostrils. He remembered how the bright silver sink barged its way into his vision of white. How the odor of the last night's seven-seven's mixed in, creating a stench worse than death. Inside his cab, Charlie touched the tip of his cheek and thought he felt the inside of his mouth. He let his face fall into his hands again. And again, for the second time in otherwise many years, he let it out as if he were five years old again.

<u>33</u>

"Deep in a Hole"

Nearly an hour had passed until Charlie was emotionally conscious enough to keep motoring. As the monster ten roared on, he felt blank in his own existence. But not enough to light another Red and force the volume of Sesame Street to double digit decibels.

But by ten PM, Charlie was back in his hole. The joy that usually shrouded around him when he was about to cross state lines was nonexistent. It was swept out of him when he tore out of the last of the major Rockies. He stared at *and* through the I-10 signs that whizzed by him every few miles and became numb because of it. He didn't know how much time had passed. He didn't even know if he had smoked a Red, nor was he positive that the battered pack in the hip pocket of his jeans contained any.

He no longer thought about any of it: Rhiney, the lot lizards, that kid they ran off the road all those years ago, or even that little piglet on the motorcycle and the fact that he couldn't pull the trigger on his legacy. Charlie simply remained in his hole, sinking deeper and deeper into his metaphysical earth. He figured he would keep on sinking until he burned up in the core. He no longer cared. He no longer needed to.

Charlie had reached stretches like that before. Once, in California, smack dab in the middle of the Sierra Nevada's, Charlie made one of the many less than savory decisions of his life. He was on his way to deliver a tanker full of petroleum oil to Truckee. Some hapless veteran was trying to convince him to drag him down one of the many steep and spectacular grades the Sierras had to offer. They both left a stop somewhere around Sparks, Nevada at the same time, and the guy had egged and taunted Charlie on Sesame Street ever since. He was mellower and his threshold was quite a bit thicker in those days, so for an hour or two, Charlie did his best to ignore him. But when the guy howled that Charlie was pinker than the lips of a virgin, he decided his pride would cash in there.

By that point, he had been driving for at least ten years, so he was quite confident in his ability. The only thing that plucked the fearful strings of his heart was that he wasn't familiar with the particular grade he and the yokel from Oklahoma chose to do battle.

At the time, Hal hadn't sent Charlie out that way much because it was one of the more dangerous ranges in the country. They were such ridiculously steep grades that were so sharp and rigid that they seem to stab the sky. Or at least big enough to poke the king through his throne up there in his kingdom.

Charlie flirted with fifth for a long time while he and the Okie stayed neck and neck down the grade. At one point, the Okie maneuvered his brand new, shiny Peterbilt in front of him and slammed his breaks so hard on a razor-sharp bend that a spring actually flew up and chipped Charlie's windshield.

Needless to say, it ended bad. Right before the road widened enough for them to cruise side by side again, their speeds had reached upwards of eighty miles per hour. Charlie hit a rough patch in his five and skidded enough to snap the lines and overturn the trailer. The Okie sailed on past him down the grade. The last Charlie saw of him was a boastful wave of the hand out his window.

Meanwhile, Charlie's trailer broke completely away from his tractor and slid into one of the Sierras sharpest boulders. Quickly, thick, protruding petroleum oil spewed across the highway in unattractive black glob. The river of oil was probably halfway to Truckee by the time the DOT bears had reached him by the roadside.

One of them churned out fire and brimstone at Charlie through his seething glare, citing all sorts of environmental and road conduct violations.

Charlie, being the hotshot he thought he was, yawned right in the man's face. The DOT bear was beyond shocked, breathing heavily through his sweaty, greasy exterior. He glanced at his partner, a bony, gray haired woman on the verge of retirement that Charlie had pinpointed as a dyke right off the bat, and looked back to Charlie in grizzled contempt. The man's head and heart lay heavy and aspartic with fury. He probably took one look at Charlie in those days and had him pegged. Charlie stared on with his slick hair, his two-day-old whiskers, his tan, firm skin glistening in the low mountain sun.

"What do you have to say for yourself?" the man asked in a lowly voice, almost a whisper.

Charlie never got the chance to answer; he merely shrugged his shoulders and spit out a chunk of phlegm that was lodged in his throat. Whether by expert marksmanship, or pure happenstance, the gob of Charlie's minerals landed right on the man's steel-toed workboot.

Charlie hadn't thought of that scene in quite some time. It had been so long ago that it only existed in his memory as a cliff note to his career. It was a still photograph floating around the grey matter somewhere near the bottom, like a piece of grime that sticks to the drain. It wasn't completely disappearing, but nowhere in conscious sight either. Now that it boldly crossed Charlie's radar, he remembered that it ended with him being laid off for three months, two of which he spent recovering in Truckee Memorial hospital after the DOT bear broke Charlie's jaw and ruptured his spleen. Charlie never counted that memory as a lost battle, frankly because he never considered it a battle at all. He was coerced into it, the Okie and the greasy bear were to blame, not Charlie.

But the months that followed that incident were the last time he remembered being this deep into his hole. He remembered lying in that electric bed, the sickly sweet smell of hospital food and bad medicine. He remembered lying there and feeling useless while his body worked overtime to recover. Meanwhile, his playground called out to him from his window, *Wheeeereee arrrrrree yooooou, Chaaaaarrrrlie?! We neeeed yooou! Weeee ahhhllll neeeeed yoooou!!*

34

"The Great Unknown"

The following day, after Tucker made several attempts to convince Aspen to join him in the trip over to Globe, he finally was able to pry him out of his office. They were driving in Tucker's unmarked car, tooling along the Old West Highway – heading east. The same stretch they had found the ill fated Charlie Coldbrick.

Signs for the upcoming Apache days littered the otherwise blank highway that connects Apache Junction and Lordsburg, New Mexico. It was clouding up a bit. It secretly reminded Tucker of the colder, wispy night he spent in a phone booth back in South Dakota, waiting for something to happen.

"So what do you think this is going to solve?" After several days of murmurs and hushed, church syllables, Aspen finally spoke on his own accord.

"I don't know. But I'm still curious to find out," Tucker replied coolly. After another mile marker or two, they passed a sign that stated Globe was a mere 20 miles up the road. "Aren't you?"

"Aren't I what?"

Tucker smiled, knowing full well his recently estranged partner heard him. "Aren't you still curious?"

"I don't know any longer. Maybe not." A silence passed between them again, it stung more than most of the quieter moments between the two. Aspen cleared his throat, "You know, I've been talking to Cindy a lot lately. Ever since I had that pissing problem. We haven't talked like that in quite some time. It feels good. Not about the case or anything. Hell, not really even about anything relevant going on in our lives at the moment. It's deeper than that. I'm still finding out things about her that I never knew. It's really quite incredible. She stills wants to go back to school. It just about bowled me over. 'What's stopping you?' I ask her. She told me that it's not knowing how it'll turn out. 'You can't be afraid of that,' I told her."

He took a break to sip out of his styrofoam coffee cup. It was brewed to perfection, three sugars and no cream, just the way he liked it.

Tucker remained silent, sensing more was to come. He could tell that his partner wasn't just sharing a pleasant exchange like they were accustomed to doing. A point lingered somewhere in the back of all that double talk. But that's about all he could sense, his mind was still reeling from the dreariness of the case. The wonder in his soul about what exactly they were going to find up at the Gila County Medical examiner's office.

"Did you hear what I told you, Desie? I said to her, 'You can't be afraid of not knowing.' That's when it hit me. If I truly believe that, then what the hell am I doing? My whole occupational identity doesn't make any sense. Neither does this. What are we even doing? Is this where we are supposed to be right now? Why do you think that we haven't gotten a hold of the doc? Why do you think the guy in New Mexico told you what he did?"

"Oh– now you want to talk about that?" Tucker shot back quickly, the temperature within him rising. "Okay, we'll talk. You know, I wasn't quite sure if anything I have told you within the last week has been registering. But you did hear me. Aren't you the least bit curious as to why the doc in Colfax claimed he had Charlie's body? We both saw that Charlie was lying face down in the sand and that he was wheeled away in a wagon that was marked *GILA COUNTY*, right? I mean, correct me if I'm wrong, we did see that. Right? We saw it. The photographer saw it. The parameds certainly saw and touched it. Plus the half dozen or so state patrol guys. So are we supposed to just accept that? We all made a mistake? Or are we all just crazy?"

"The feds haven't asked about it since it was in its second week."

"That's because they don't care. I mean, we aren't even dealing with a homicide. They have more important things on their agenda. No one cares. So we have to care. Have you forgotten that? Don't talk to me about 'not being afraid of not knowing.' Everyone is afraid. We figure it out so that we are less afraid. That's what we do. If you don't want to do that anymore, that's fine. But I have to know."

"Don't **you** wonder about this Charlie guy. No one knows him. The two that we interviewed only met him once. But I saw something on both of their faces. The first time I ignored it, because I wasn't going to let myself believe a kid that had just been in an accident and who might be suffering from brain damage. But don't you wonder about people like that? There are hundreds if not thousands out there. I have a brother in Kansas City. Did I ever tell you that? No, I don't think I did. He cut off everyone from his life.

I haven't talked to him ever since he joined the army. I don't even know if he still is in Kansas City, I don't even know if he's anywhere. Maybe people like that do that because they know they were meant for something else. You must think about a bigger picture sometimes, Des. You ever think about what's outside Gila County? Outside Arizona? Outside this world in general? I know you're not religious. I'm even talking about outside of religion. Maybe we aren't supposed to know what happened to this Charlie guy. You can't be afraid of that."

"We are going to find out," Tucker grumbled, speeding the car up when they hit a straight stretch.

He wished desperately that he wasn't involved in this conversation with his partner. Secretly, although he would never admit it aloud, he was wishing he hadn't asked Aspen to join him at all. As the last few miles whizzed by, he decided not to even look at him. The man sitting beside him was a stranger. More of a stranger now than ever before. The truth is Tucker had to find out. The truth is – Tucker *needed* to find out. And not Bradford King, or Darryl Aspen, or Gila or Colfax County was going to stand in his way.

"I don't know, Tuck." Aspen kept reiterating, "I just don't know. I'm coming along with you, because I know how important it is to you. But I have no will left for it myself. Chief gets back the day after tomorrow. I'm handing him my resignation. I'm getting out of it."

And if you were smart, you would too.

"So that's it?" Tucker was becoming calmer again, but he still sneered out the corner of his mouth. This ultimate betrayal to their partnership, their limited friendship, their streak; it was eating him up. But he thought it might be best not to show it.

Not until I find out.

"That's it." Aspen nodded.

<u>35</u>

"Into the Vale of Tempe"

He drove on– silently– faintly listening to the words of wisdom his playground had to offer. He thought about the yellow haired bunny on the bike. The picture of her fragmented remains spewed across that highway like the petroleum oil never left his mind. It only temporarily aborted when his playground reiterated the long lost words of the Okie.

You're pinker than the lips of a virgin, Charlie.

Charlie drove, but his heart remained forlorn. As Deming gave way to Gage and Lorsburg, he took a bit of solace in the fact that he was about to cross the final line. The Old West Highway into Arizona. Into the vast land of sand and cacti that surrounds his final destination…TEMPE. He hardly noticed that the goddamn glorious ball of fire rose once more in the sky, searing his leathery flesh, and stinging his pores with sweat.

When Charlie couldn't eliminate his many enemies, he often pretended they weren't there. And when that didn't work, he took action, usually the trigger happy kind. More often than not, it usually landed him with another black mark on his record. It did when he tried to ignore the badass in Council Bluffs, as well as the Okie in Truckee.

It was happening to him again as well. That picture of the beautiful pig on her cycle, rose higher and higher in his mind, it turned his skin redder, and somehow grayer. It was that smile that Charlie couldn't peg.

Why was she so goddamn nice?

Charlie figured that she too had a motive, a plan of action, but like him, she too couldn't get the deal done. Was it because she really had somewhere to be? Or did she take pity on him? It all goes back to that smile on her face, that smile was the single most impenetrable mask Charlie had ever come into contact with. Was she laughing at him behind closed doors and close quarters with the one who needed her most? Did she regail the tale of crazy old Charlie Coldbrick? If so, was it done respectfully, or merely as some sort of amusing lark? Did she describe the hideous piece of rot that continued to eat away at his face?

These were all questions that floated through Charlie's mind, in some form or another. As the pure, white hot light of the San Simon Valley tried to slow Charlie and his monster ten, he figured how he could no longer ignore this particular enemy, citing the same reasons and rationalizations as before. Before his mix-up with the yellow haired philistine. Before he had to go and drudge up old memories of black oil eating away at the concrete red carpet to Truckee. Before he had to go and analyze every aspect of everything that ever went wrong.

Of course, he thought. Why else did the word jump out at him so many times before. It was on his papers, the very papers that she had made a point of checking up on. If Charlie had been more focused on the situation instead of his own conundrum, he might have found it odd that she checked his papers. That right there was one clue.

The DOT pigs could givea flyin' fuck to where yer goin', they only ever check the logs and she didn't.

But what could that mean?

The word even had forced its way into his dreams, dreams of *Death* Valley, and hot colored sand that was manipulated by the whispers of his playground. Hoping that the clues and messages it was trying to send wouldn't be lost on the hard headed likes of Charlie.

What did that mean? What was Charlie's world trying to tell him? What was going to happen in…

TEMPE?

As Charlie drove on, trying to fit the pieces of this awkward puzzle together, he grew more and more tired, but his mind was still operating on some kind of emergency level. He had no idea of how time had passed because time was impossible to plot along the wayward, snake turns of Highway 70 through Safford and eventually Globe. Instead, he thought more about getting his legacy back on track. He felt his hand gently graze the contents of his pocket. It wasn't his intention to reach for a Red, he had run out of those long ago and no longer craved them enough to stop. He had promised himself no more sleep and no more relief. Instead, he found his fingers aching for the touch of the stainless steel buck that sat smirking in his pocket. It sat, waiting for the chance to kiss the cool fresh, night air of…

TEMPE.

That was where it was supposed to happen. That is what Charlie figured the message was supposed to be. The end of the road. The last stop. The final destination. The venue of his recently revamped legacy. Surely there would be plenty of DOT pigs waiting for him at the terminal. The only question that awaited him when he got there was which he would carve like a thanksgiving turkey first.

When he pictured them waiting, bored stifless, twirling the chains in which their many keys hung from, whistling nameless tunes, he smiled for the first time in ages. Plastered on the snouts of all of them were the greasy exteriors of that bear in Truckee. Sweaty, half-amused mugs that were just begging for some action.

When you come right down to it, all them bears look the same. They look at you like it's their playground. But while they're sitting in plastic cages and hollowed out terminals, enforcin' it, I'm out there, livin' it.

Charlie wondered what kind of nazi organization would try to control something so wild and beautiful and untamed as the open road.

When I'm through with them, all the other tractor jockey's will be thankin' me. They'll look up from their clusterfucks and wiggle wagons and say, that there's a guy who's got it right. *Once the news hits on Sesame Street, maybe they'll observe me a kind of silence, like they would any hero who died for somethin' they believe in. Somethin' everybody believed was right, but no one had the guts to say.*

He thought about the ones who knew him, Rhiney, Hal (wherever he is) and yes, even ever so briefly, Darla the dyke. The first two Charlie figured would not be surprised of his untimely end. Somehow, all his life, everyone who had ever met Charlie figured his end was right around the corner, but they might not have known why.

As for Darla: *Well,* Charlie thought, *she would be right to thank her lucky, carpet-lickin' ass that I was all the way down here and not up there. Cause if I was anywhere near Sioux Falls, I woulda made a Darla-que a priority.*

But Charlie remained calm, as he passed a scattered pile of bones of some kind of giant desert lizard, much too giant to live in any other world but Charlie's, he realized that Globe was coming up soon. "Won't be long now," he whispered back to his playground. "Won't be long now."

<u>36</u>

"Happy Hour at Gerry's"

The only features worth noting in front of the aging white stucco building that housed the offices to the medical examiner's staff was an American flag whipping clumsily in the wind, and a ten story radio tower off to the east. Other than that, most men who had spent only a little bit of time there would agree that it looked much like the rest of rural Arizona. Unobtrusive flat and salty rocks littered the landscape along with the ancient skins of the reptiles and the dried up basins that once resembled bodies of water.

Inside, Tucker felt the last of the summer heat follow him in. "So," he asked the woman who held down the fort at the front desk, "Is he in today?"

"You're back, huh?" she asked, smiling in an almost unabashed, conspicuous Morman fashion.

"Yes, I'm back," Tucker snapped. The conversation with Aspen in the car earlier had him riled– he was still choking on the news his soon to be ex-partner had fed him. "He can't hide from me forever."

"He is indeed in, but he's with someone at the moment, if you just want to wait –"

But Tucker had something else in mind, he marched off into the direction of the coroner's office, leaving the secretary to give her spiel to Aspen.

She looked only a little stunned, but the strange smile never left her face. Glancing at Aspen, she gave him an almost sympathetic look, like she could sense some kind of pain he was in.

"I apologize for my partner, he's been under a lot of pressure lately. We both have."

"You look like you're doing okay," the smile on her face grew wider.

"I am now," he winked and followed the fast path his partner took into Favre's office. As he pushed his way through the half closed door that had a sign posted on the handle reading *fughitaboutit*, he heard that Tucker was speaking civilly enough to Gerry Favre. He stormed in as a hurricane, but something must have stopped him cold in his tracks, because he was a calm cloudless spring day when Aspen found him. Neither party had acknowledged him entering, nor was there anyone in his office as the secretary had suggested.

"– you remember what you said, right?" Tucker asked in his calmer, interrogative voice. "You said, 'There's no way in hell that man died last night.' I believed you then and I really believe you now, Gerry. But you have to help me, because I can't figure this out by myself. What really happened to this guy? Colfax County said it was the melanoma. Is that true? You have to tell me. And I want to see him. I never really looked at him under the sheet that day. That's another thing, I want to see him for myself." Tucker's calm weaved back into a rant as his eyes danced wildly amidst the thick, stale odor of stogies that embalmed the room.

Aspen watched, almost mesmerized as his partner hopped from one foot to another. Tucker was trying desperately to regain the composure of the old detective that solved so many cases in a row. But the sad fact was, and it occurred to Aspen in a very subtle and unobtrusive way, neither of them were the same after this one. The truth is, no one who had gotten any sort of breeze of this case had seemed the same. Even Gerry, who he had only met maybe two dozen times in his life, looked a bit more aged and out of it than he normally did.

"Take a seat, Mr. Tucker," Gerry said in his grandfatherly voice. "I'll pour us a drink."

Suddenly, Desmond seemed to catch himself in the frantic light the other two had been watching him. He tried even harder to compose himself. He slumped his shoulders and lurched forward around the coroner's desk, and took a seat next to his soon to be ex-partner.

"Hi Darryl," Gerry gave him a halfhearted salute.

"Hello Gerry," he tried to smile as best he could, but was still probing Tucker as if he were under a microscope.

Gerry took his time, but eventually lined up three straight glasses in a row like he was tending bar at Los Alamos. Next came his tired reach for the crystal glass that housed more than enough bourbon for the three of them.

"Are you sure that's a good idea?" Aspen asked, glancing at his watch. He was beginning to feel better and better, now that he let his partner in on his five-year plan. Secretly, he was wondering why he was denying the drink at all. Somewhere down deep, he figured it would have been a nice capstone to a mostly commendable career.

"For what I'm about to tell you…yes, I think it is completely necessary." Gerry didn't bother to look up while he poured each glass a third of the way full.

"So you do have something?" Tucker asked, still frantic and frenzied, but regaining his serenity back.

"Oh yes," Gerry handed Tucker a glass first, then Aspen his. He took a swill out of his own, "I have something all right. Don't know if it's what you want to hear, but I can tell you if you like."

"Anything can help." Tucker's eyes grew wider at the possibility of finding the piece he was looking for.

"Okay, here goes," Favre huffed as he crashed back down into his old wooden wheelie chair. He took another deep swig, and sighed.

Aspen looked around his ancient office. It looked about as old and moldy as the man sitting before them. Half packed boxes and files were scattered about the room. He was trying to remember the last time he saw Gerry.

Had it been five years? Ten?

He couldn't really be sure. They hadn't had too many cases with a body recently. And when they did, they were usually over in Claypool, not Globe. The day they found Charlie, he had apparently missed him by a couple of minutes because he was traveling by bus back from Tonto.

Tucker had seen him. He wasn't sure, but he figured his partner would have let him in on it if he noticed something was wrong with the medical examiner. Something was definitely amiss with Gerry Favre, he just couldn't put his finger on what.

"Bout three weeks ago, the wagon rolled up and brought in a cadaver, the name on the tag read, Charlie Coldbrick. That's your man. The report requested a tox be done, because of the circumstances in the discovery. So, and let me remind you that I've been doing this for forty some odd years, I didn't think nothing of it. I shuffled him to the back of the line, we had a lot of bodies that week. Lotta accidents. Did you hear that one about the parents who poisoned their kids?" he shook his head sullenly. "Don't know what folks are thinking about sometimes. I never would want to be in your fella's boots, or at least that's what I used to think. But after staring at the aftermath for so long, I don't know if I want to be in anybody's. Not anymore. I don't know, maybe I've been doing it all too long. Maybe I've been working up to this point for some time now." He took another long swig.

Tucker, fidgeting beside Aspen cleared his throat and opened his mouth, but no sound came out. Aspen thought maybe he had lost his nerve, or less likely, maybe he forgot what he was going to say.

Gerry responded by putting his hand up, "I know, I'm getting to your man, Charlie. Long story short, the week after he came in, the Mrs. and I took a holiday for the weekend, went and visited her cousins in New Mexico. I come back and step into my work, I had a few people left before I got to your man. Anyway, it was one Wednesday ago now, I open up the drawer, and he ain't there. He's gone. Poof." Favre brought his hands together and then pulled them apart with open palms to simulate that he vanished, as if into a plume of smoke.

"Gerry-" Tucker started.

"No, before you get going, this had happened once before. In that case, it turned out the family didn't want the tox anymore so the meds came back and brought the body onto the funeral home without so much as a memo to me or my staff. But I thought it was strange, because on the report there was no next of kin listed. And since it was your office that enlisted the tox report, I thought it doubly strange. But I'm a calm man, and more importantly, I'm a logical man. If something's missing, I think real hard about the last place I might have seen it. Well, obviously I don't frolic with the bodies late at night or anything of that sort, so the last place I remember seeing your man was in the drawer where I left him. To be honest gentleman, someone else could have taken it, but Lois out there said no one came by while I was gone on holiday...except you Mr. Tucker. I usually don't get too many visitors out here.

"I can honestly say to you fellas with no uncertainty about it. This is the single most disappointing moment of my career, and I haven't had many. I always prided myself, but when you get a blotch like this coming along...well, I can see the writing on the wall. My wife says she been tellin' me for years, maybe it was just something like this that needed to happen."

Aspen smiled at Gerry, he couldn't remember the last time he had even seen the man, but he suddenly gushed with admiration. Gerry had just reiterated everything he had said to Tucker in the car, and even more so, everything he had been telling himself for the last several days. He figured they shared a similar pain, brought on by the mysteries of this case, and the easiest thing for both of them to do was to let it go.

Of course, Tucker refused to see it that way. The frown and furrow he wore on his face said it all too well. "Let me just see if I have this straight Gerry. You're telling me that someone took his body. They stole it right out from underneath you? They pulled a Dr. Frankenstein?" His eyes were wide and wild, like he was contemplating lunging at the medical examiner right across his desk. He hadn't even touched the bourbon the good doctor had set in front of him. It's as if he was stuck in some other kind of world where only the truth mattered.

"What I'm telling you, Mr. Tucker, is that he just disappeared."

A long and awkward silence entered the room where the three sat and stayed there. It was as thick as the stale cigar smoke, all three of them could sense it, like a vapor in the air. With each passing moment, the tension grew thicker, almost toxic.

"Fellas, I can't tell you how sorry I am. And I know I haven't been exactly forthright about this, avoiding your calls and such. The truth is, I didn't know what to tell you, because I was ashamed. I'm ashamed because I never have been this careless toward anything. But I don't have an explanation for you. The body is gone."

After taking a small sip of his bourbon, Aspen was the first to respond, "That's okay, Gerry. These things..." He didn't know how to finish that sentence. He nearly said, *these things happen.* But that wouldn't be true. He hadn't had as long a career as the man that sat across the desk from him, but it was long enough to know that these things didn't just happen.

They don't happen at all.

But you can't be afraid of that, Aspen thought and smiled.

"Something is going on here," Tucker sounded calmer, but his face was sweating bullets, and his hair began to snarl and curl on its own. "I want to see the empty drawer. Show me the empty drawer! You hear me, Gerry? I want to see the empty drawer and then I'll go away!"

Aspen stood up, he could see that his soon to be ex-partner would not go quietly.

"There's nothing to see there, Mr. Tucker. He just disappeared."

"Don't you say that to me! Don't you say that to me!" he screamed. It didn't seem like he was even screaming at Gerry any longer. He was screaming at something past him. Past everything. He was screaming at something outside of the building. He was screaming at something outside of Gila County. Outside of Arizona. Perhaps he was even screaming at something outside of the world. It took every bit of Aspen's strength to peel him out of Favre's office and drag him back to the car.

<u>37</u>

"A Sign from Above"

The sun had long disappeared under the horizon again when Charlie saw the first road sign for Tempe. It didn't glimmer and emit a thousand watts of light like it did in his dreams. Actually, it said, "Mesa / Tempe / Phoenix, follow Hwy 60," but its message was all the same. It was a few minutes from midnight when he passed the easily forgettable village of Miami, Arizona. Soon the dark blanket of desert sky, illuminated with a thousand blistering, winking lights that reminded him of the flickering ashes of his Reds, would give way to some kind of errant civilization. The sneaky, desert sticks would morph to desert suburbs. Shadows of palm trees tracing over sandy sidewalks, people walking every which way in their thronged sandals and khaki shorts, enjoying the all-too-brief, merciful, cool summer night.

Soon, hellfire on wheels will be makin' its way into this haven of illegal tacos and down and dirty derelicts, and they won't have the slightest idea until it's too late.

Charlie smirked as he studied the map he threw onto the passenger dash all those weeks ago. When he fled the Dakotas in a storm of confusion and white hot pain. Now the calm and collected eye of that storm was positioning itself smack dab in the middle of Maricopa County, waiting for its chance to sound its war-cry. As Charlie steered the dusty ten along the outskirts of the San Carlos reservation, something popped inside of him.

It wasn't the dark, cloudy moonless night that surrounded his waiting coffin, although if there was an official town called *the middle of nowhere*, Charlie was certain that what he was looking at would be on the postcard. Nor was it the sound of crowing vultures circling high up above, making their voices heard over the thundering diesel engine droning in tenth. It wasn't even the soft, nearly invisible clouds that drifted waywardly as if they were leading a funeral procession. It was none of those things.

Instead, it was something up ahead, sticking out of the road. It was too high to be a mile marker, but too sloppily placed for any God or Forest Ranger to have planted a cactus seed. It was another road sign, in between mile markers where no road sign should be. The murky headlights of the ten weren't even close enough to graze it when Charlie watched the bright white letters leap out at him. They seemed to attack his eyes and render them useless.

He stabbed the breaks and held onto the steering wheel with one hand, while the other fumbled inside his pocket out of pure, unbridled instinct. His tires screeched and dragged rubber across the highway in a brutal fashion. Once he realized they were mere letters on a sign, that they weren't tacos or DOT Bears or any of his other enemies jumping out at him, he relaxed both hands and drew off the brake pedal quickly. His heart ran a marathon around the galaxy as he passed the culprit, a wayward sign that was pounded into the hard desert earth with a wooden stake.

The sign read: *TEMPE.* It had an arrow pointing up.

The speed at which the road– along with the earth– cruised along seemed to have slowed in an instant. Charlie took a deep, gaping breath and soon became afraid that it would be his last. He relaxed his foot off the brake pedal, but it seemed impossible to find the gas or the clutch. The tainted ten slowed to a stop all by itself, as Charlie cursed it in a wistful, hindered breath. He wasn't quite convinced that something had malfunctioned under his panicked red hood, because when he rolled to a stop, the engine continued to grumble in its low, intimidating voice. The rpm needle jumped whenever Charlie's foot would find the gas, and then lose it again.

It was pitch black out, but Charlie felt the *need* to shield his eyes from some unknown blinding source of light. He glanced over his surroundings through soggy, teary eyes. There was nothing but dark shadows that grew darker the farther away they were. He saw their undefined ridges prodding the darkness almost subconsciously. Mostly, because all that his mind allowed him to see was the word that branded itself permanently across his line of sight…

TEMPE.

He was sure that he was still a good sixty miles from it, and had figured earlier that he wouldn't arrive until around the time bartenders across the land were screeching, "LAST CALL FOR ALCOHOL!"

It's wrong. It has to be a mistake. Some scatterbrained, redneck road huckster drove that sign in a bit too goddamn early. Must'a been the bastard's first day. Didn't even get it near a mile marker.

But somehow, someway, that sign calmed Charlie as much as it frightened him. It terrified him because he wasn't even sure if it was actually there. He felt something pop in his head moment's before, perhaps the sound of one's mind snapping. He felt lighthearted and lightfooted, as if he had been in some serene, drunken seven-seven binge for days, only his mind was still lucid. The crisp desert air wafted in from the crack of his window, letting in the smell of life. It's as if the sign had eradicated every last waking and overanalyzed moment of the past several weeks. He no longer heard the whispering of his playground, tickling his ear and scraping his mind. Only the gusty, fruitful, nightly breeze remained.

<u>38</u>

"Believe in Angels"

Lonely hours followed detective Tucker wherever he went in the days following the visit to Globe. He did manage to calm himself, but his vigilance in solving the case had remained the same.

There was one aspect of it he did accept. No longer would he be getting any new information, because the chief barred him from investigating any further. The probation stemmed from an incident two days after Globe when he attempted to reach the first witness, Abby, several times by telephone at her mother's residence. She had been discharged from the hospital, but still healing when Tucker dialed her number. The only thing he got out of her was *he saved my life*, then her mother came on the line and told him to stop calling.

She must have complained to the department.

However, he was allowed to pour over the old case notes to see if he had missed anything. And pour over them he did. He read and re-read every one of the chicken scratched scribbles he and his ex-partner had made in their notepads. He devoured the uninformed fed report, and listened closely to the interview they had with Darla several times over.

Nothing seemed to jump out at him. Just a few phrases from his notes that kept creeping back into his mind at random times of the day.

He just disappeared.

...saved my life...

I hope there is only one of that asshole.

if you were smart, you would too.

can't be afraid of not knowing.

There were times when he could toss everything aside with giddy glee, and times where he thought he would have a nervous breakdown if the answer didn't come to him.

What's so wrong with trying to find the truth?

No one understood him any longer, or so he figured. Even his contemporaries skipped their daily visits with him in his office. Not one of them asked him to lunch, or asked about the wife and kids. No one could comprehend his obsession. *After all,* they would tell him, *this is just a job.*

Tucker wouldn't listen. Even the chief, who he always felt he could depend on and respect, told him to wrap it up, he wanted the final report on his desk no later than Friday. When Tucker pushed the issue, the chief responded, *sometimes you just need a fresh start*.

They were lonely hours indeed.

His wife took the girls and went to stay at her Mother's place up in Flagstaff, she had been gone nine days already. Tucker wasn't sure if she was coming back. His clothes were wrinkled, smelly, and they no longer creased. He had resorted to eating frozen TV dinners, and the lawn hadn't been mowed in over a month. Worst of all, he missed his partner – he missed Aspen.

The notion would have been laughable a couple of months earlier, but Tucker realized after Aspen had departed how they kept each other in check. Like everyone had been telling them all along – they were the perfect balance.

Their exchange on Aspen's quitting day could only be described as civil, nothing more. That too could have been the reason so many of his co-workers had given him the cold shoulder.

Aspen was well liked around the department; he was a man of faith, a good listener, very humane, and always made time for the other investigators in their unit if they needed to chew the fat for a while. Tucker had always been viewed as more stoic. While his reputation was always deemed professional, he just couldn't relate as easily because he wasn't as personable. But no one had held it against him until that moment.

Then there was Charlie.

Tucker often closed his eyes in his office and tried to imagine what the man was really like. Was he the beer swilling, loud, abrasive red neck that Darla made him out to be? Or was he an angel, walking the land a few extra days to save and watch over the world as Abby had indicated?

Did she indicate that? Is that what I really think?

Tucker couldn't be sure. He wasn't sure of anything anymore. His whole being felt like it had been turned inside out and hung up to dry, rendering him impotent in nearly every aspect of his function. But orders were orders, and he planned to follow the chief's because that was his job. He would write his final report, then he would be done with it. He would join the others and let it go.

The streak is over.

Under normal circumstance, the final investigative report would follow a tight outline in order for it to be admitted into the case file. But Tucker figured out long ago that the Coldbrick case was anything but normal. There was nothing usual or run-of-the-mill at all about what had

been going on. The routes and channels they took, the way information had

slowly unfolded to them. As Tucker tried to recite the road to where he

currently stood, he became dizzy and had to change the channel. One thing

popped out at him as he did so. Something he told his wife a couple weeks

previous. He admitted to her that he didn't believe in God, even though they

had exchanged their marriage vows in the presence of a small Lutheran

church on the opposite side of town where they lived. He told her he didn't

believe, but that something was working against them.

So instead of the usual title, aim, method, results and conclusions

that would fit the mold of a standard file report, Tucker thought instead he

would write the chief a letter.

To whom it may concern,

*For the past six weeks I have been investigating the death of one
Charles W. Coldbrick. He was found along side the highway next to
an upside down pickup truck in rural Gila County. This case has been
a nightmare. The jurisdictional messes and complications between
departments my recent ex-partner and I encountered while
investigating doesn't even begin to describe the trouble. We received
conflicting accounts on the victim's personal character, and vague
and unclear stories from witnesses. This has been the most
disappointing case of my career, bar none. It brings to light some
serious doubts on my abilities as an investigator and maybe even
more so as a human being. I know you were likely expecting an
investigative report, and although I have written my fair share over*

the years, I would have no idea what to put into this one. I can tell you what I think happened to this Charlie, but even that changes on an hourly basis. Forget it – I actually haven't the foggiest idea what happened to the man. I have no idea who he was, what he represents, or where he is now. I don't know if he ended up in the desert that day because he was just unlucky, because his death was timely, or if he was part of some greater plan. I recently told my wife that I didn't believe in God, how can I when there is such craziness in this world? Maybe I don't know if that's true or not, but one thing I can say is that someone was with that girl when her pickup did a swan dive into a bed full of rocks in the middle of the night. If it wasn't this guy Charlie, then it was some stripped down version of him. Maybe we didn't find anything on him because he had already repented to whatever higher power is out there. Maybe an act of God is what confuses those of us left behind to pick up the pieces. A good man I knew once told me, there is nothing wrong with the unknown. I guess there are things we shouldn't know in this world. Either because we can't comprehend them, or it would be much too reflective. Please don't take this letter as an indication that I too am tendering my resignation. Mr. Darryl Aspen had his own reasons, and I didn't realize until now that those reasons are his own and can only make sense for him. Also, please don't take this letter in a way that I have flown off my rocker, for I am about to make one the sanest and most humane decisions of my life. Something that has been a long time coming. So before I let you go, let me apologize. I failed the department and I failed myself. But a lesson in humility is a very valid one, and it should not go unnoticed. If it had, then I wouldn't be much of a detective. I will be back and anxious to meet and greet whichever partner you see fit to assign me.

Warmest regards,

Desmond D. Tucker

He gently sloped up from his desk, feeling weary of the evening twilight. Inquisitively, he wondered how long he had been working on it, or maybe more appropriately, what time he started. He tore the pages out of his typewriter and folded them three times. He then stuffed them into a manila envelope and took a walk down the hall.

It was just past six p.m. on a Friday and the office was nearly abandoned. A few of the rookies were chatting it up near the break room, and the night janitor was going about his work at his usual frantic pace. Everyone had somewhere to be, including Tucker. As he listened to the sound of his boots clack against the hardwood floor, he realized it was over. This would be the last contribution he would make to the Coldbrick file.

So why did he suddenly feel so good about it?

He entered the chief's office warily, but still knowing he would be gone. The office was littered with pictures of his family and decorations and accolades galore. There was a black knit sweater hanging on the end of his wheelie-chair. An oscillating fan hung lowly in the corner that was sure to blow his papers all over the place once activated. Tucker gently placed the manila envelope at the center of the desk and gave it a good pat before he left again.

Back out in the hall, he pondered it one last time.

Maybe both accounts of his character were right. Maybe he had to watch over that girl as a penance to how he lived his life before.

It was no more plausible than any other scenario the detectives threw out the night they were spitballin' in Sioux Falls.

A veteran he hadn't noticed was still present popped out of his office, a fella by the name of Duke Barlow. He had come to the criminal division six years previous. Tucker's relationship with him had been by no surprise to many, purely professional. "Hey Dessie," he called out to him in a chipper voice.

"Hey," he responded, still feeling a weird vibration in his soul about how he left things with the Coldbrick file. Feeling even weirder that Duke wasn't giving him the cold shoulder when so many of his colleagues had.

"Smile man, it's Friday!"

Charlie Coldbrick, guardian angel.

"I know it is."

Charlie Coldbrick, overseer of the unfortunate and applying God's love to all he encounters.

"So, do you have any plans this weekend?"

Is that really what I believe?

"Yes, I do."

No.

"Oh yeah? What?"

"I thought I would drive up to Flagstaff."

But that there is a start.

<u>39</u>

"Asleep in the Desert" (reprise)

Charlie decided to exit his cab. Normally, he never would have pulled off the highway like that. Let alone set foot out onto an area he wasn't familiar with in the middle of nowhere. But his head was spinning in such revering semi-circles he felt he wasn't able to drive at the moment. He decided to keep the truck going. It also occurred to him that he was long overdue for a break, even though he promised himself he wouldn't.

Even Charlie's so called legacy was the furthest thing from his mind. He couldn't get that sign out of his head, and his legs told the rest of him that they had to make sure it existed.

As Charlie ambled out of the cab, he collapsed to the ground in an unspectacular fashion. A muted throbbing shot out of his leg like a silent alarm. Although, the pain didn't seem as bad as it should have when one falls nearly five feet into gravity's hands.

Under the few dim, ruby colored lights of his trailer he saw a shiny piece of metal bounce off the ground and roll somewhere under his cab. Right around the same time, he heard a soft *plink* that suggested something hard and heavy fell onto the road.

Dazedly, he searched the contents of his pocket, even though he was already sure of what he lost. True enough, everything was in its right place, with exception of his trusty buck. He figured it must have taken a tumble from his jeans when he crash landed onto the asphalt. What surprised him the most was how indifferent he felt about it. He was just taking it as it came.

What about your legacy? A fierce, horrified voice that was losing its power droned out of the current gust. Charlie remained static in the strangely comfortable, albeit painful position he had landed. He gazed up at the sky and remembered far off days when he would watch the same set of constellations saunter across the ether as he sucked on a Red from atop of his metal throne. He remembered how those days felt, how not necessarily this desert, but within many like it he would feel his most free. It was on nights like these that Charlie Coldbrick truly felt he had found his corner of the world, and no one could take it away from him. But something interrupted his lapse...

TEMPE

"Ah shit," he groaned as he carefully helped himself to his knees. As the blood poured out of his head, he felt the balance shift once again. Suddenly, his hand was aimlessly grasping at the dusty ground under the cab, in search of the only scepter he ever knew. He felt a spot of oil that had leaked out onto the sand, something prickly that only could have been a cactus needle, and some kind of hardened mud that seemed to form in clusters on the road. But he did not find his buck.

"No," he sighed, as he stood upon his legs for the first time in hours. They were wobbly, as if they were made of jell-o pudding. He took a few steps and heard something creak; it felt like one of the bones in his leg was starting to splinter. He bawled out at the night sky as if it had done him a terrible injustice. The leg he held groaned along with him, his other knee dropped to the ground and he nearly lost his balance. Instead of his body, he used his hand to break the fall and positioned himself to stay upright.

He stood up, slower this time; he quickly cast a glance back down under the truck, hoping his buck would wink at him through the darkness – like the stars were. When it didn't reveal itself, he thrust forward, determined to find out why this unscheduled layover had presented itself.

After ten or so steps, he began to feel much better. The calm breeze dried out the protruding sweat that lined his face, leaving only a greasy shadow behind. After a few more minutes of walking, he looked back and could no longer see his truck. He thought he heard a slight hissing sound that reminded him of rattlesnakes, but then realized it was only the turbocharger acting up on the ten.

As astounding as it seemed, try as he might, Charlie could not picture how far the sign was from where his playground had stopped him.

What was it, then? Two feet? Twenty? Ten-Hundred-Fuckin'-Thousand?! Where are you, Charlie?! What's your twenty? You're lost in every sense of the word. Don't matter though, good-buddy! No one will ever need *anything from you.*

"TWO GODDAMN MINUTES! IT WAS TWO GODDAMN MINUTES AGO!!" Charlie screamed out of pain and frustration at an empty desert basin. He shut his eyes and squinted, he was so desperate that he would have glued them shut if it would have helped. But the only thing he saw from between the first glimpse he caught of the sign and when he stepped out of his truck was that word again.

TEMPE

It looked just as ominous as it did on his papers the day Darla shoved the keys to the ten in his face.

Just a word, a goddamn word can't hurt ya, something deep inside him tried to rationalize.

"Didn't think Death Valley would hurt me neither..." he muttered under his breath, countering the voice.

Doesn't matter – when you go to sleep, they're one in the same. Is that why you won't go back to sleep, Charlie? Getting' tired, good buddy? You ain't in TEMPE yet.

As he limped on, he was able to ignore the last remnants of his playground, just like he was able to back in the old days. The same way he was able to fend off the Okie's taunts when they were skirting down the mountain, at least for a little while.

Charlie stopped when he could no longer hear the ten behind him. Not seeing it was one thing, but not hearing it was too much to take. Besides, no shadow of any post had revealed itself in front of him, and he felt something else slowly carving its way down his face. It wasn't sweat, it was too thick. It felt almost like syrup, which Charlie figured meant blood. That thing on his cheek had exploded again, only the casualties were much greater this time.

He streamlined around and started back the way he came, careful not to put too much weight on the leg that had become more painful than his face.

When his legs stopped after a few paces, he glared down at them as if to ask, *What the fuck you doin'?*

They refused to answer or work any longer. In a brief moment of sheer insanity, Charlie believed his playground was stopping them like it had stopped the monster ten. He thought that it was preventing them from going any further until he promised he would make good on his legacy.

He glanced back upward and something caught his eye. Had Charlie blinked at the right moment when his head swiveled back to where the ten stood, he would have missed it entirely.

Somewhere off in the distance in the black hole of the night, something was floating...something red. Charlie's heart instantly began to palpitate irregularly at the sight of them. Two dim, little stars, twinkling reservedly in the darkness. They were side by side and they seemed to be shuddering in identical movements. They almost seemed to be calling out to Charlie, *We neeeeeed yoooou! Please coooooome! Hurry! We neeeeeed you!*

The voice was different than the one his playground spoke in, it was much more alert, urgent. In a way, Charlie figured it almost sounded like a siren. He blinked heavily, all he could see besides the murky red lights was black. It would be sugarcoating it to say his breathing was irregular, Charlie was huffing like he had just hiked up Pichaco Peak back in Red Rock.

Now he wanted nothing more than to get back to his cab, but at the same time, the two imperative, yet seemingly harmless, floating lights were comforting, almost kind. He took a few steps into the direction of the lights and shuddered. In a sudden burst of chilled wind, he felt the flowing river on his forehead harden and stop all at once. He took a few steps closer and the lights separated a bit more. Charlie doubled the amount of steps he took, until his legs cried *ho* and he thought he may have heard the sound of hooves scraping the ground off in the distance.

At least he could hear the ugly ten sounding off in its grumbling voice again. But it was quieter and coming from an odd, diagonal direction, which wreaked havoc on his senses. An equal amount of steps later, the lights grew to be about two feet apart. Their growing made a noise that sounded like soft moaning.

Heeeeelp me Chaaaarrrlieeee, I neeeeeeeed yooooooou.

A few steps closer the lights grew even further apart, and the sound of his ten was as good as gone. The moaning was louder and it was accompanied by a low whining sound. Charlie squinted in the darkness, trying to filter out the rest of the sudden noise. He thought it sounded like one of those tiny, pathetic engines from one of those Japanese manufacturers. Charlie once heard a man on Sesame Street call them *Rice Rockets* and figured it was pretty close to accurate. He also figured he was far away from the road, because he couldn't even see the dim, mostly burnt out lights of his trailer. He looked in all directions, it was all blank, dead space – with the exception of the two round lights staring back at him in their ever widening gape.

As he took another brave set of steps, a smell joined in with the rest. It was the smell of smoke, a charred mineral of some sort. Charlie's sense of smell had been pretty much shot when he once filled up a beer can with gasoline and stood right over it as he dropped it into a bonfire. Not to mention all the years of Reds. But regardless, this same damaged sense told him it was the smell of burning oil.

The moaning remained, it sounded helpless, as if it didn't know why it was moaning. It was the sound of a shattered voice droning on fruitlessly.

One last set of steps later, Charlie was able to solve the mystery of the floating lights. Tail lights actually. When he reached out to touch the round, dim twinkles he felt warm plastic and the sound of a whining belt about to snap close by. He hobbled around to the side of what felt like a metal frame being stained by black smoke and reached for an opening.

It was again as if his hands had a mind of their own as they aimlessly clawed at what Charlie figured to be an unnatural addition to this or any desert. But it was darker out than the deepest part of the hole he had sunk into earlier. Charlie's hand was stuck between the door and a thinner piece of metal that could have only been a handle. There was only one problem, it was upside down. When he tried to jerk his hand around in the opposite direction, he heard something crack.

Now Charlie's cries once again filled the borderless wasteland he stood in, they overtook everything. The earth seemed to shake at his bellowing. He felt the need to puke his very skeleton out of his body and collapse to the ground in a puddle, but he couldn't quite get there. Out of pure instinctual rage, his foot lashed out at whatever had attacked him, it connected with a smoother, slicker substance that sounded like a shattering window pane when his boot fractured it.

When he stopped, the soft moaning remained, only a bit more sure of its purpose now. Charlie took his left hand, turned it upside down and almost instantly found the handle. He pushed in the plastic button and threw open the door, causing brighter, whiter lights to flash out at him.

The light was dim, but blinding all the same. For a moment he felt his ears pop and heard sound flow in and out. The lights pulsed in unison, their power source fading. Quickly, Charlie's eyes began to adjust, and he saw that the light created a jagged semi circle surrounding him. He felt like he was under a spotlight, like whatever twisted power that had thrust him into this situation was now in the front row gawking and laughing hysterically.

What had presented itself to Charlie was a brown, Ford pickup truck ravaged and hurled upside-down. The light allowed him to pierce the darkness slightly, but neither the road, his ten, nor any other car was in sight.

Another pair of twinkling lights stared back at Charlie, blinking and wincing rapidly along with everything else. They belonged to a bloodied young girl, all of about sixteen. Her face was one big bruise, her nose was revoltingly bent to one side and the dashboard had been caved in so far that her knee was stuck in its grasp.

Her eyes, a light brown, looked like they were twinkling because they were stained with dew. They were also dancing at the sore sight of Charlie.

The girl's lips parted and a tiny river of blood flowed out and into her eyes, staining her lids pink. It crept down her forehead and created a thin, sticky stream in her hair.

Charlie hovered over her, and strangely, she never looked away. She looked like she was trying to move her arm to reach out to him, but it didn't budge more than a few inches. A croaking noise was trying to break out of her throat, but it seemed she didn't have the lung power to give it that final push. She was still breathing, she was also still buckled to her seat.

Charlie peered around the inside of the cab in a daze. A shooting star of fire ambled through the innards of his leg, cutting the meat. He gasped as the sharp, white pain spread itself out like a spider's web. His eyes began to sting as if tear gas was sprouting out of the engine that was still running, albeit on its last leg as well. What Charlie could make out was a bunch of clutter that must have spun around like a tornado after the initial impact. But it was hard to tell what things were on account of everything was upside down.

More dizziness shrouded Charlie and he collapsed to the ground at the foot of the overturned truck. On the way down, he split his bottom lip something awful. His chin had connected with a long, lanky piece of metal sticking out that had peeled away from the truck's roof. As he lay on the ground, the voice of his playground came back as if the speakerboxes were locked tightly inside of his head.

What are you doing here? This is none of your business. That girl's as good as dead! You will be too, if you hang around much longer! She's not worth it! Nobody is, Charlie! Mind your own business, Coldbrick!

When he finally was able to help himself up again, his leg had twinged a final time and was then rendered useless. He was no longer able to control it, it almost seemed to hang off of him lifelessly, like a dead limb of a tree. When he fell he landed on his face, which now seared in agony. He looked back down at the girl, and she didn't look any better, in fact, she looked worse.

She was barefoot, but an upside down bag of shoes laid half spilled out behind her. Her blouse had ripped at the belly, more blood peered out of the hole in her stomach.

"Jesus," was the only thing that was able to escape from Charlie's lips. He started to wonder if he could even crawl back to his truck. And, if he did get there, would he even be able to drive it? A thousand more questions weaved themselves in the inner fabric of his mind, until a nonsensical sound chortled out of the girl's ruby, red mouth.

"Help me," she was able to correct the sound in a low voice.

Charlie studied her face closely since she was addressing him. Until that moment, he had made a point to not look at her. Maybe because she wouldn't want him to, the more he let his face rot away these last few weeks, the stranger and sparser the looks from others had become. But she stared right back at him, fiercer than what would have been expected for a girl practically young enough to be his granddaughter.

Her eyes looked chilled and full of fright, almost like they would shatter like a mirror if Charlie were to reach out and touch them. Her nostrils flared as one of them blew a blood bubble from the river protruding from her mouth. A few of her teeth were missing, but for the most part she had kept her lips tightly together.

"Help me," her voice shook, "please."

Charlie continued to study her. His mind was like a jumping jack firecracker that protests in a haze of fire and smoke as its being pulled in all directions. For a moment, he thought about how painful and long it would be if he tried to run back to his truck and drive away. Another notion that his mind presented him with was what would he do if he still had his buck? Would he revise his legacy once again? It would be all too easy. He would also be doing some guy around the same age a massive favor by taking the shit she'll put him through right out of the equation, or so a part of Charlie figured.

As he looked at her, his playground whispered, *Just gonna grow up and mass produce while sucking the life force out of every man in sight. Just gonna be another lyin', cheatin', misery spreadin', man controllin' bitch. Hell, I'm sure she broke her fair share already. If she lives, she's just gonna keep on mowin' em' down. She's gonna mow em' down like all those diesel daggers you've been drivin' mow down and shred the highway to smithereens.*

Charlie remembered how he thought the blonde-bunny, evil knievel would look if he scattered her pretty parts all over the highway. But the image slowly changed in his mind. For a moment there was black, then he saw the girl in the overturned truck. She was no longer upside-down and leaking vital bodily fluids. She was a picture of health. Her flesh was cream colored and facilitating a nice tan. She stood there, standing with a hand on her hip, her distaff, proportionate frame positioned like a lamppost in the middle of the desert highway. The cool, soft breeze making her hair dance and point and tease and torture what she was standing over. Below her perfectly pedicured, pink painted toes was a whole slew of victims. Men and boys, old and young, all torn to shreds in a hasty, yet premeditated, merciless display of genocide. She stood there in Charlie's mind and stared right back at him, pausing to smile at the carnage she had created. She twirled a pair of oversized sunglasses between her fingers and whistled a nameless tune that nevertheless stood all of Charlie's errant hairs upside-down.

When he closed his eyes to erase the horrific image, he no longer saw black. Instead, he saw the steaming, crystal clear Mohave. With the buzzards circling up above and his very own brown, young body shriveling up like a burnt fuse on a stick of dynamite. His focus shifted to the red, mars-like terrain below the chariot he laid upon, all by itself. The old familiar whispering of his playground commenced and tiny, lucid letters popped up out of the sand like a jack-in-the-box. They spelled out –

"Please, I need you to help me," the girl's voice wavered like flame in a wind storm.

Charlie opened back up his eyes and forgot about everything else. "What?" his voice grumbled and croaked from under-use. "What did you say?"

"Please mister," new tears flowed over the old ones that stained her cheeks, still puffy from swelling and an inkling of baby fat. The last remaining remnants of childhood right there, reminding everyone who gazed upon them of more youthful, innocent days.

"I need you to help me. Pleeaassee." Her voice was becoming more desperate. As if Charlie was someone who wasn't able to understand her words and she was using all her effort just to communicate the message to him.

With that, something else broke somewhere deep inside Charlie. It wasn't his face, that was still numb along with the rest of his body. It was something else. Something that Charlie was able to ignore up until that moment. Something that had been trying to bite and claw and fight its way to the surface, but just learned how. It was something that offset everything else. It was some kind of antidote, an inverted substance that neutralized everything in its path. A kind of brightness that wasn't painful at all.

The picture of her standing over a thousand bloodied victims bubbled over and melted away, as if the photo paper had been under an intense heat.

Do you even know what a legacy is Charlie? People remember all sorts of crazy things. It's amazing what trivial incidents stick into the minds of others. People can't remember the combination to their luggage, but they'll always know where they were the day Kennedy was shot. They forget loved one's birthdays, but they'll remember that story in the news of the

farmer that won the lottery and was able to fight off the foreclosure bankers.
They can't bring themselves to cry at the funeral of some far off relative, but
they'll always remember to laugh when their child falls down after taking
the first of many steps.

Yeah Charlie, people remember all sorts of things. Some things they
remember better than others. This girl could be a ravenous monster that the
world would best be rid of. She could be. She could get pregnant, live off
your taxes and raise degenerate offspring to follow her lead. She could pass
over many wonderful people in her life just to get to the one who really
doesn't need her at all. She could lie, steal and cheat to get ahead. She
could exploit people's weaknesses and use them against whomever she
wishes. She could use people to her advantage and then toss them out when
she's through with them. She could bring them to believe anything she
wanted. She could weave them a fantasy that couldn't possibly last. She
could make them feel like they can't live without her, until one day, they'll
have to. She could leave a lot of bodies in her wake. She could move onto
the next, and the next, and the next...sucking out their very existences.

She could do anything she wanted.

Why, she can be anything right now. She's probably something. She's probably somebody's daughter, sister, cousin, friend – lover even. She probably does things for them that no one else can.

Nobody knows what she'll become, least of all you. You don't know if tomorrow is the day she'll save somebody's life. You don't know if she'll cover someone's shift even though it's her day off. You don't know if someone goes out of their way to be near her, to make their day just a little bit brighter. You don't know if the world seems a little bit more hospitable to that person, just because she's in it.

You don't know if it's her mission in life to keep the populous, popular. You don't know if ten years down the line, she'll yearn for a whole new set of responsibilities. The kind that keep the world spinning. You don't know if one day her children look to her for the only answer, because she could be the only person who knows the right thing to do. You don't know if she's the only person to keep them warm, to hold them safe. You don't know if she's the only person to be able to help rebuild what others have destroyed. You don't know if she's the last one left of her kind.

Bottom line, Charlie. You don't *know.*

"Please Mister," she continued on, "I feel light." A smoldering, blood stained tear trickled down her scalp, moistening the dried up river it traced.

And what about those that need her most? There is absolutely no substitution for who she will be to them. She could be the one who gives them something to look forward to. She could be the only one who fits perfectly with them. She could be a muse to some fruitful Apollo, she could teach them things they thought they never wanted to learn. Someday she might be there to rescue them in ways they can't possibly imagine. She could keep the fire burning inside them, hotter and longer than any kerosene or gasoline. She could be another heartbeat around the house. She could be someone to take care of. She could be the most beautiful thing someone ever lays eyes on. She could change their whole world at first glance and never let them go back. She might even be the last person they would ever have to meet. She could have a hundred different smiles and a thousand different laughs. Her presence could be their ideal representation of home.

"Would you hold my hand?" she reached out a burnt, skinned arm to Charlie. "Please hold my hand. I need you to hold my hand." She continually repeated her unanswered request until Charlie repented and took her cold and clammy palm into his. She squeezed tightly to make sure he understood her dire *need* for survival. To make sure he knew she understood his as well.

She could be anything she wants to, Charlie. Soft, firm arms to hold us while we're sick. A soothing voice to talk us through our most chilling nightmares. A soft breath on the back of our neck to cool our internal struggles. A hug that convinces us to do the sensible thing. A whisper that defines and makes sense of the rest of the world. A presence that reminds us that we're alive. An open mind to confide in. A power that makes the impossible, possible. An observant set of eyes to watch over us, just as you are watching over her now.

Do I believe that? Charlie asked himself when the voice faded away.

"What's your name, Mister?" the girl, as if she had been listening along with him the entire time, asked.

Do I think that's true?

He met her glance and did not turn away, "My name is Charlie."

No –

"My name is Abby."

But that there is a start.

"Tempe"– comes from the "Vale of Tempe," near Mount Olympus in the sovereign nation of Greece, a land haunted by Apollo, the Muses and other Gods.

This book was begun on January 1st, 2007 and completed October 13th, 2008.